To Mom

Infinite Monkeys

Lloyd Rahani

Brian Homer

PUBLISHER'S NOTE

This is a work of fiction. Any resemblance to actual people living or dead, is coincidental.

The authors would like to acknowledge:

Thanks to Tarquin for being a perfect muse and to Lloyd for urging me to keep writing when my writer's block seemed immovable. *Barbara Hower* (aka babsy55)

I would like to thank everyone in the Anthology for their support with special thanks to Tim Yao and Katherine Lato for their supervision and planning throughout the process. *Sabrina Lato* (aka Bookgrrl)

To my wife Rae, for her love and encouragement. *Mike Manolakes* (aka Horatio)

Thanks Melodie for letting me take Novembers off. *David E. Dean* (aka trrdedean)

I wish to thank my wife Nan and daughter Kristiana for their support of my pursuit of my writing dreams. Many thanks as well to Katherine for editing Infinite Monkeys and for keeping us all on the path to a successful completion of the 2009 Pledge. *Tim Yao* (aka NewMexicoKid)

Thanks to my beautiful and talented wife, Maria, for all her support and encouragement. *Timothy Paulson* (aka tireddadx3)

I dedicate this to Sheeva and Thor, my dogs, who passed on to a better place after I finished The Scapegoat. I thank Whiskey, for surviving and being my best friend when I need one. *Patricia Wigeland-Clemmons* (aka sheeva)

Thanks to Barry, for everything and for always, and to Jacob, Elishabet and Sabrina for their support and encouragement. *Katherine Lato* (aka KatherineWriting)

I would like to acknowledge that certain things are true, and among these are the truth that I would not be here (in this book) if not for the incitement and encouragement of my family, especially Katherine. *Barry Glicklich* (a.k.a. Finbarr McG)

Thanks to Barbara for her help and patience and teaching me where the commas go. *Lloyd J. Rakosnik* (aka Grayraven)

Thank you everyone who has faith in me - Ky and Pat Ostler and especially my father Jim Ostler. *Tom Ostler* (aka tomster)

Author Index:

Dedication:

This book is dedicated to Tim Yao and to all the people who contribute to NaNoWriMo.

HOW TARQUIN CAME INSIDE, MET BASTET, AND LEARNED TO PRAY AT THE IRON CATHEDRAL

by Barbara K. Hower

That August day turned out to be the watershed moment in Tarquin's life. But he wouldn't know what a momentous day it would be until some time later. It was a day like any other in his short life—he was out and about, playing with his sisters and brothers, and one of his aunts was watching them while his mom, Greta, was out getting meat for dinner. Tarquin loved feeling the wind caress him, and he seemed oblivious to all the traffic noises and the grumbling roar of the freight train as it lumbered down the nearby tracks. He barely batted an eye as a neighborhood kid on his motor bike rattled down the street, sounding like a giant, annoying mosquito. He and his siblings were totally focused on playing as hard as they could. They ran and jumped and rolled around until they had to sprawl out in the lush green lawn and catch their breath.

Later that afternoon Greta had planned to give the kids some more hunting lessons. But before the lesson could take place, Tarquin and his siblings got sidetracked. They stopped and sniffed, their heads bobbing ever so slightly and their nostrils flaring, and began to track the source of the aroma. Inside the wire object sitting on the lawn was a bowl heaped high with tender, flaky tuna and all of them went to investigate. Then WHAM, a door slammed shut on them. Unbeknownst to them, the two-legger with the caterpillar on his upper lip had been sitting quietly behind a mound of peony bushes. He leapt out and quickly slammed the door shut. Tarquin, his siblings, and aunt panicked and began flailing and scrabbling about madly, trying to find the way out...but to no avail. They were trapped!

Before this August day dawned, Tarquin's life was a mix of structure and abandon—established times to learn new skills and hone existing ones, yet lots of time, too, for running, playing, and wrestling with his siblings. All of his clan members were born in a garage—just like the legions of others in his large extended family. Tarquin was a cat born to Greta. Queen of the Feral cats, she ruled the neighborhood with an iron paw, casting a watchful, slightly cross-eyed, gaze over her dominion. In her world, cats lived without human intervention and two-leggers were viewed with suspicion, if not outright hostility. Oh, they were good for providing food and water, which helped supplement their diet of rodents and birds, but two-leggers were not to be trusted.

The ferals loved the life they lived. They were like wild little weeds, growing and spreading rapidly in their realm. All they knew was life in its wildest state. The ferals just concerned themselves with things they could see, touch, smell or taste. They relied upon their senses and seemed to have a heightened sense of awareness. They came and went as they pleased, unencumbered with the rules and restrictions their domesticated brethren had to deal with. But because they chose to live outside in the wild, they didn't live as long as house cats did since cars, other animals, fights, and disease took their toll. However, right now they were thoroughly mortified that they had let a mere bowl of tuna sidetrack them. They should have seen that two-legger.

Before the great trapping day, Clair, the female two-legger, had noticed there were cats running about in her back yard and mentioned it to one of the neighbor ladies. The neighbor, Charlotte, was in her mid-sixties and solidly built with a page boy haircut, and she was wearing khaki shorts, white ankle socks, and sensible shoes as she puttered in her yard. She reminded Clair of an ornithologist—all she needed was a pair of binoculars slung around her neck and a bird book tucked under her arm "Oh yes," Charlotte said sweetly, "they're feral cats. God's little creatures. You can't touch them, they're wild, don't you know. But we love them."

Clair quickly wrapped up her discussion with Charlotte and strode purposefully back to her house. Joe, the male two-legger, who was just settling in to watch some TV, looked up when he heard the door slam behind Clair.

"I met one of our new neighbors," Clair said, with a grim smile etched on her face. "Her name is Charlotte and she's nuts! Apparently we have a colony of feral cats around here and Charlotte thinks it's God's will that they just keep breeding and growing in number."

Joe looked up, grabbed the remote, and muted the TV. He knew he was going to be hearing about these cats for a long time. Clair was crazy about cats. They had just moved into this house, an old place built around 1900 and which had undergone a series of not-so-effective renovations. It had been a rental property for a number of years and the landlord clearly wasn't interested in keeping the place up and was biding his time until he could redevelop the property into a McMansion. The roof shingles looked like they had a bad case of sunburn, peeling up and flying off at the slightest provocation. The large deck out back was as uneven as country road. But it was a good cat hideout under that sloping expanse of deck.

"What do you propose to do about this cat situation?" he asked Clair, his voice assuming the soothing, calm timbre he used when Clair was getting upset. "Sounds kind of tricky if they're afraid of humans and you can't even catch them."

Clair leaned against the doorway by Joe, with her arms crossed in front of her and her jaw set. "I guess the first thing is to make sure they have food and water," she said. "Then maybe if we gain their trust we can figure out a way to trap them and have them neutered."

For the rest of the rest of that year, Clair dutifully put out bowls of dry cat food and fresh water. Mom cats and their little baby balls of fluff would show up on the back deck. Moms would eat and then stretch out in the dappled sunlight and nurse their babies, their little heads butted up against their mothers' bellies, tiny paws kneading away contentedly as they suckled. Then Charlotte would emerge from her house two doors down and start "kitty-kittying" and doling out food by her back door. The cat troops would perk up their ears and then race through the high grass next door and over to Charlotte's where they would swarm around her as she plied them with food.

One cat in particular seemed to be the supreme commander. She was jet black and if any human came too close, she would glare and hiss. Clair named her Greta. "You know," she laughed at Joe, "like Greta Garbo. She vants to be alone...or at least left alone!"

The following spring, Clair noticed there were a few less cats around. Most of the missing cats were adult males, but one of the females that had begun to look a little ratty was also gone. But Greta had made it through the winter and four of her female kittens were now old enough to have babies of their own. One day a cat would look like she had swallowed a bowling ball. Then the next day she'd be sleek again, and Clair knew another litter of kittens had entered the world. Almost all of the kittens would be jet black, with an occasional steel gray one thrown in for good measure. Then a yellow male showed up and some tortie kittens began to appear, flaunting the yellow markings of dad.

During this time, Clair volunteered at an animal shelter as a cat socializer. She had talked to the people at the shelter about her feral cat problem, but was disappointed when they told her there was nothing they could do. Too wild, too unmanageable, and too dangerous. No way would anyone want these cats. They also explained that unless you can get a hold of kittens before they're eight weeks old, they usually couldn't be socialized to humans. And the feral mom cats were very careful that none of their brood got within easy reach of the two-leggers.

The August morning that Tarquin and his kin were captured, Clair was socializing cats. She was working particularly hard with one long-haired tabby cat that was terrified of being in the shelter and cowered in the back of her cage. After six weeks of working with Tabby, talking softly to her, and crawling into the cage with the cat, Tabby was finally becoming more at ease with humans, and the terrified look had left her eyes. A staff member came and got Clair, telling her she had a phone call. Puzzled as to who could be calling for her at the shelter, she picked up the phone and said "hello."

"You've gotta come home right away," a clearly excited Joe

shouted into the phone. "I've caught Greta and the four kittens. In the dog cage we set up outside."

"Great! I'll be home as soon as I can," Clair replied. This was, indeed, wonderful news. At the very least maybe they could get these cats neutered. But deep down Clair was hoping she could try her hand at socializing these feral cats. She hurriedly finished up at the shelter, hopped into the car, and sped back to the house. She felt like her feet weren't even touching the ground as she ran over to the cage where Joe was standing and looked at the seething, writhing mob of angry cats inside the cage.

"That's not Greta," she declared as she looked at the cat who clearly wanted to rip her to shreds. "That's one of the aunties… but the others are Greta's kittens." The auntie was a solid black cat, about six or so months old. The kittens—one solid gray, two solid black, and one black with a white spot on its chest— appeared to be about three or four months old.

"That's ok though," Clair said. "At least we can get these guys neutered and maybe we can get homes for them. If not, we can release them back into the neighborhood. But they won't keep reproducing."

Clair and Joe found a low-cost spay/neuter clinic and took the reluctant felines in for their surgeries. The neutering and inoculating completed, Clair set up the cage in an outbuilding on their property and dutifully went out many times every day to feed them and socialize them. She had named them all: Sammy, Gracie, E.Y, Rondell, and Delino.

"They're so cute," Clair thought as she observed her new feline family. "And so wild."

"Ok, here goes," "she muttered as she opened the cage door and reached her hand in. "It's ok. I know you're scared. It's all so different than what you've ever experienced, isn't it?" she crooned soothingly to the kittens.

Sammy and Rondell hissed and swatted at her. E.Y. just cowered in the corner, trying to pretend she was invisible. And Gracie arched her back. Her favorite, Delino, sniffed her finger and licked it. His little black nose just barely grazed her finger and his little kitten tongue tickled her finger. She smiled and felt a flicker of hopefulness course through her body. Maybe they were tamable.

A couple of days later Clair was weeding in her garden. She had left the door to the out building open and noticed that Greta was ambling up the sidewalk toward the building. A limp, lifeless chipmunk dangled from her mouth. Clair watched, intrigued. Greta warily walked into the building, turning and glaring daggers at Clair. The kittens ran up to the side of the cage as she walked in, calling to them with a churring, guttural trill. She looked at them for a moment, and then dropped the chipmunk by their cage and left.

Clair wiped tears from her eyes. Evidently Greta wasn't done teaching them. But she was smart enough to figure out she couldn't get them out of this predicament. If only she could let Greta know that her babies were safe.

The next day was bright and sunny, a breeze with just a hint of coolness to it. Clair put on a pair of jeans and her favorite Cubs tee shirt, grabbed a cup of coffee and stirred in some cream, and went out to the cat house, as she and Joe had begun referring to it. She pulled up the red vinyl-covered kitchen chair that had somehow ended up in the corner of the outbuilding and sat down.

Sipping the coffee, she watched the kittens through the rising steam from the cup.

"Today we're going to try being held," she announced to the kittens.

She unlatched the cage, the door grumbling metallically as she opened it, and reached in. Delino was right there, so she grabbed him. She gently scooped him up and set him on her lap. He looked up at her and she was elated when she realized there was no fear in his eyes. As she touched his little sides, she could feel a faint vibration. She picked him up and held him to her ear. He was purring ever so gently. She gave him a tentative nuzzle and a quick kiss on the top of his head and put him back in the cage. Invigorated by how well this exchange went, Clair reached in and picked up Rondell. It didn't go as well. He panicked and launched himself back into the cage and raced over to Sammy and tried to burrow underneath her to hide.

"Ok, I'll take my victories wherever I can get them," Clair chuckled as she watched the kitten's attempt to be invisible.

That night she excitedly told Joe about her breakthrough with Delino. "I'm telling you, that kitten understands that I'm not going to harm him and that I'm his friend. We made a connection…stop laughing at me, Joe! I tell you it's true. He seems curious about me and we're interacting." Clair folded her arms in her familiar "don't-mess-with-me" stance. Joe liked cats alright, but he was really a dog person. She knew he thought she was a little daffy when it came to all things feline.

Joe laughed, his eyes crinkling up at the edges. "I didn't say a thing! I think it's great you're making headway with the one." Joe stood up and walked over to the bookcase, straightening an old tattered book that had slid over tipsily against its neighbor. He turned and looked at Clair. "I was going to suggest that we keep Delino."

As Clair looked at him dumbfounded, he added: "I talked to a guy at work today. He has a friend in Iowa who has a dairy farm. He thinks they might take a couple of our little orphans."

Clair felt a rush of gratefulness overtake her. Joe amazed her sometimes. Here he was, trying to find homes for these little guys! This was great news, as she had talked to a friend, and when she had heard about Clair's new cat family said she would take two kittens.

"That's fantastic!" she said as she rushed to hug Joe. "Jane said she'd take two of them as well. That means they'll all have homes."

Joe laughed. "Now the only hurdle is how to introduce Delino to Lucy and Brilly. They won't like having a kitten underfoot."

"But you know, Delino needs a better name," Joe said. "I know you named these guys after Cubs players, but once the real Delino gets traded—and you know he will--will you be happy with a cat named after an ex-Cub?"

"I've been thinking: why don't we name him Tarquin?" Joe suggested. "In 'Horatius at the Bridge' by Macauley there's a line: 'Lars Porsena of Clusium, By the nine gods he swore, That the mighty house of Tarquin, Should suffer wrong no more.' It's a neat name. And that cat just reminds me of a little panther, kinda noble and all."

Clair smiled. "I like that name. Besides, there's a Monty

Python sketch with a Tarquin character—the Silly Party
candidate: Tarquin Fin-tim-lin-bin-whin-bim-lim-bus-stop-F'tang-
F'tang-Olé-Biscuitbarrel."

From then on Delino was Tarquin. The cat seemed to like the
name, too. Clair moved him into a spare bedroom that contained a
small, red convertible couch, a chair, dresser, and a cat perch.
Tarquin would scratch at the wooden frame of the perch and then
bask in the sun, watching the world unfolding beneath his gaze.
Thinking that Tarquin would miss his littermates, Clair had
bought him a little stuffed pink pig that was almost his size. He'd
grab it with his teeth and drag it around the room with him, and
when he got tired he'd snuggle up against the pig and go to sleep.
Every day since the other kittens had gone off to their respective
new homes, Tarquin seemed more at ease with Clair and Joe.
Tarquin was about six or seven months old by then, still definitely
still in his kittenhood, but filling out and assuming the shape of an
adult cat. Clair would take a book into the room and sit and read.
She felt that her presence helped Tarquin feel more confident and
secure. Now whenever she walked into the room, he would make
a series of little squeaking meows and run up to her, grab her legs,
and nip at her ankles. She giggled as his sharp teeth strafed her
legs. "I know that's a term of endearment," she told Joe after the
first time it happened. "That's what my mom's cat does to her. I
think that means I've passed the cat quality control test."

Really, Clair knew that Tarquin's actions toward her meant that
he had made the transition from being cat-fixated to being human
fixated. This point was driven home the first day she introduced
Tarquin to her two old lady cats—Lucy and Brilly. Lucy, who
was the mother of Brilly, took the lead role and started hissing
menacingly at Tarquin. Brave whenever her mother was nearby,
Brilly joined in and began hissing too, only her hissing efforts
ended in an undignified snort. Tarquin's amber eyes widened

when he heard the cat cacophony and looked over at Clair. "Why
the potty mouthed outbursts?" he seemed to be saying. Finally, he
ran over to Clair and sidled up as close to her as she could.

"You stay with me, little guy," Clair said as she stroked his
sleek black fur. "They'll come around eventually. They're not
used to kittens, that's all." Tarquin crawled into his two-legger's
lap and curled into a little ball and purred himself to sleep, feeling
safe when he could feel and smell his new human mother.

The Lucy and Brilly hissing episodes eventually subsided and
they settled into an uneasy truce. They all ate together, three little
melamine cat bowls lined up on a plastic mat sporting the image
of a cat barbequing a mouse on a grill. Tarquin loved to roam
around the house and explore. He learned that stairs were fun to
run up and down, explored bathtubs and couldn't figure out any
good use for them, decided that beds were fun to hide under, and
discovered that TVs made a lot of noise and flashed a lot. But his
most favorite place was the wood-burning stove. It somehow
seemed mysterious and incredibly alluring. Tarquin also noticed
that his female two-legger had a statue of a black cat that was
wearing gold hoop earrings and an elaborate golden scarab
necklace. Brilly noticed him staring at the statue and told him
"That's Bastet. She's a really old Egyptian deity who protects cats
and the people who care for them."

"Wow, a religion that's all about cats," Tarquin thought. "That
could explain the voice I hear that isn't coming from my two-
leggers. That's Bastet talking to me! My cat mom never
mentioned any of this." He sat quietly and tried very hard to
listen and see if he could hear the voice. Tarquin stared off into
space, unblinking. It was almost like trying to tune in a
recalcitrant old tube radio, but finally Tarquin received his

instruction from Bastet. Go to the cast iron cathedral and your prayers will be realized.

Tarquin assumed a reverential position, crouched in a sphinx-like position in front of the cast iron wood-burning stove, and prayed very hard. "Oh Bastet, please send me a juicy bird," the little cat beseeched the Egyptian deity. Soon he heard a fluttering, flapping sound. His ears pricked up and his eyes grew large in amazement. There sat a dusty brown sparrow that had tumbled down the stove chimney and sat looking about, confused.

"Wow, I never thought my prayers would be answered so quickly," Tarquin thought as he reached over and grabbed the bird in his mouth. "Ooh, it tickles my mouth."

He trotted into the living room where Joe and Clair were sitting. "What's sticking out of Tarquin's mouth?" Joe asked. "Oh my gosh, it's a bird," Clair exclaimed, leaping to her feet. "Come here Tarquin, give me the bird, sweetie," she cooed.

"Go catch your own darned bird," Tarquin harrumphed as he raced up the stairs. The bed seemed like a nice spot for the bird, so he carefully set the stunned, and now sodden, bird under the bed. "Drat, here came the two-leggers," he said to himself, and watched sadly as Joe scooped up the bird and escorted it outside to freedom.

Tarquin went back down to the cast iron cathedral and began channeling Bastet again. Just like the last time, another bird tumbled down into the belly of the stove. This time Tarquin placed the bird gently behind some books on a low bookcase at the head of the stairs. Seeing the kitten heading upstairs with another telltale feather sticking out of his mouth, Clair followed and instructed Joe to close the stove's door to stave off any further bird escapades. She pulled back the blue dust ruffle of the bed and peered underneath. Except for a few dust bunnies she had missed in her cleaning, there was no bird. Tarquin had joined her by now and was helpfully looking under the bed with her.

"What did you do with that darned bird?" she asked the cat. Looking at her with a gleam in his eye, he made a couple of chirping sounds and trotted off. As Clair started back to the stairs, she stopped.

"That sounds like a bird," she mused. Looking around, she finally decided the sound was emanating from the bookcase. She gingerly pulled back a book, and perched in the bookcase was a befuddled bird, cocking its head and chirping its confusion and unhappiness with its current situation. Again, Joe did the honors and deposited the bird in the Juniper bush outside. Lying in bed that night, Joe and Clair laughed as the thought about their day of birding.

"It was almost like the cat was praying at that darned wood-burning stove like it was a church," Clair laughed. "Maybe it's some cat religion we don't know about—the church of the blessed birds."

"If it is a religion," Joe commented, "you've got to admit Tarquin's sure has tangible results. He prays for a bird and 'hey, presto' he gets what he prays for!"

About a week after the bird incident, Tarquin saw Greta while his male two-legger was feeding her and darted outside. Greta looked at Tarquin briefly, but then ran to the neighbor's yard. Evidently he had too much of the human about him now. Suddenly realizing he was outside and overwhelmed by the outdoor noises and the wide openness of it all, Tarquin darted under the deck. Clair ran outside and lay on the ground, trying to entice him out with a variety of cat treats. One time he was about to head toward her when a train went by and scared him. Tarquin bolted back further under the deck and stared out at Clair. It was so dark under the deck she could just barely make him out—just the little white smudge on his chest showing her where he was. As he glanced around the underside of the deck where he had spent his early days, Tarquin was surprised at how shabby it seemed. At it was sure cold and damp under there. As he was surveying his surroundings, he heard a familiar sound. His female two-legger had hooked up the can opener near the back door and started running it. Summoning up his courage, Tarquin emerged from under the deck, and darted back into the house.

Tears of joy streamed down Clair's cheeks as she swooped Tarquin up in her arms, burrowing her face into his soft, fur, and feeling his skin radiating warmth. Because the weather was starting to turn colder, his fur had a crisp cleanness to it—almost like clean laundry whipped dry by a sharp, cold wind. Drying her tears, she turned to Joe. "Thank God for the electric cat caller. He knows when he hears that sound he's going to get a can of tuna."

Just then a motion outside caught her eye. It had started to snow, light fluffy stuff dancing and swirling around the deck. "Boy am I glad we got him in when we did," she said to Joe, laughing nervously as she spoke. "Otherwise I'd be lying on my belly, getting coated with snow." She paused for a minute and then said what had been scaring her while she had been trying to lure Tarquin out from under the deck. "I was sure we had lost him. That he'd go back to his former ways and take up with his outside cat family."

Joe nodded. He looked over at the little black cat hungrily wolfing down the tuna that Clair had spooned into his bowl as a reward. "You know, Tarquin had a choice just then," Joe said. "He could have chosen to go back to his feral ways, his former life. But he chose to come back to you. So he's not a feral cat anymore. He's seen and lived in both worlds and realizes that what he needs is here with us inside."

Infinite Monkeys

FRIENDSHIP

by Sabrina Lato

Michelle was talking to Samantha, her new friend, as Lisa walked to her locker. Feeling a pang of longing for their old friendship, Lisa tried to tell herself that their friendship was over. It didn't work.

Lisa unpacked her books, running mentally through the list of classes in the new semester and what was needed for each one.

"Hello," Anne said as Lisa walked up.

There's as much shown in what is said as what isn't, mused Lisa. Before Michelle had started hanging out with Samantha and Monica, Anne would always ask "Is Michelle here today?" knowing full well she was. Sure, it got annoying, but at least it had been a testament to the then-new friendship between the three of them.

"Did we have homework in Language Arts?" Anne asked.

"Yeah. You're supposed to read to page fifty-eight in King

Arthur."

"Ugh, that book is so boring."

"Yeah, but we have a quiz in it today," Lisa answered as she closed her locker. She smiled at Anne's face, and headed off to Math for the first period of the day.

* * *

Walking to her seat in science, Lisa accidentally bumped into Michelle. Michelle glanced up, and there was a flicker of recognition in her eyes.

"Sorry," Lisa muttered.

"Whatever," Michelle turned and walked to her seat. Lisa followed Michelle for a moment with her eyes, then turned and walked to her seat.

"OK," the teacher said, walking to the front of the classroom. "I don't want to hear any talking, because your test on mixtures is tomorrow, and I expect perfect scores out of all of you. You're my best class, so let's see if we can do this!"

Lisa opened up her science folder, but she wasn't concentrating on the words. She was remembering when they'd chosen their current lab partners. Back at the beginning of the year, when Lisa and Michelle had been assigned to the same science class, they'd been thrilled. Their enthusiasm had only increased when the teacher said that she would be giving them a chance to choose their lab partners starting the third quarter.

By the time the third quarter had rolled around Michelle had become concerned about being popular. When Samantha had approached Michelle and asked if she wanted to be her lab partner, Michelle had accepted. She hadn't even thought to give Lisa a "Sorry-but-what-can-you-do" glance. Instead, Michelle had given her a "Isn't-this-the-best-thing-ever" glance.

That might have been the beginning of the end of their friendship. If Lisa had known it was coming, she would have tried harder to preserve their friendship.

It's over, she reminded herself, forcing herself to focus on the notes in her science folder. After all, we're expected to get perfect A's.

* * *

Lisa was washing her hands when Nancy and Eliza came into the bathroom.

"Did you hear about Michelle?" Nancy asked Eliza.

"What about her?"

"About her and Samantha? And the whole-"

"That? Of course I heard. It's all over the school."

"She's really overstepped her bounds this time." Nancy paused and looked directly at Lisa. "Can I help you?"

"No, sorry," she said, leaving. Michelle and Samantha had a fight? And it was all over the school. Lisa tried to keep herself from smiling, but it was hard. She had given up hope of their friendship returning the way it had been, or even at all. Even so, the news cheered her.

Trouble in paradise. Lisa knew she wasn't supposed to find glee in another's problems, but it was so satisfying to know that Michelle might, at least for a little bit, be wishing for her old friendship with Lisa and Anne back.

Most of what Lisa knew about Samantha came from rumors, but there was one thing that the rumors all agreed on. Samantha had a way of winning arguments, and if she got mad at you, you were generally on your knees begging for mercy within half an hour.

It was a fate that one wished to avoid whenever possible, but it was also an implied part of friendship with her. Michelle had known that full well, but she'd still chosen Samantha over Lisa. It hurt, and a part of Lisa enjoyed knowing that vengeance would be served, even if it wasn't by her. Besides, the whole incident would be over and forgotten about by seventh period.

* * *

Lisa went through her mental checklist of classes again. She'd had Math, English, Social Studies, Science, Lunch, and Home Ec, which would bring her to Gym. Joy.

She slammed her locker door shut, then headed off to the locker room. She walked quickly as she passed Michelle's locker. It was a habit from when Michelle had first started becoming "popular." For a while, Michelle would try to make conversation with her. Lisa had gotten tired of awkward conversation, so she'd tried to avoid Michelle when possible.

Eventually, Michelle had gotten the hint, so she'd stopped

trying to start conversations. Thinking back, Lisa preferred awkward conversation to no conversation at all.

Lisa changed into her gym clothes, then headed downstairs to the gym. Standing around alone was awkward, but it was better than arriving at the gym late and being marked tardy.

As she walked into the gym, the first thing she saw was Samantha. Double-joy. Gym and Samantha. What could possibly be better?

Samantha was talking to someone who had the look of I've-heard-this-before-but-I-should-listen-because-I-don't-want-to-get-on-her-bad-side. Curious, Lisa walked a little closer.

"But she totally meant it," said Samantha. "She said 'Sorry' but you could tell it was a totally fake apology. Worse than that, it was a sarcastic reply. She is so totally over."

"I know. Who does she even think she is?"

"So now my shirt is totally ruined. The teacher offered to let me go down to the gym and change into the gym uniform. As if. I'd rather go around smelling like frog than wear this a moment more than I have to."

Now Lisa was curious. Someone spilled frog juice on Samantha? Being able to manage that was impressive. Sure, they'd probably be booted to the lowest ranks of popularity, but at least Samantha would smell like formaldehyde for the rest of the day, and probably never be able to wear that shirt again.

"In your spots everyone!" the gym teacher shouted, and Lisa walked to her spot, still thinking about what she'd heard.

* * *

Lisa was starting her homework on the kitchen table when the phone rang. She paused a moment, then resumed her work when someone answered it.

"One moment," her mom was saying to the phone. "Lisa, it's for you!" Lisa sighed, put down her math book, and went to the phone.

"Hello?" Lisa idly glanced at the next problem in the book.

"Please don't hang up on me, but-"

"Michelle?" Lisa looked up sharply.

"I'm really sorry how I treated you, but I really need someone right now, and if you could be with me I-"

"So what am I, the backup friend?" The words came out before Lisa had a chance to think them through.

"Please..."

"What?"

"I... I just... please..."

"What."

"Michelle, I don't have all day."

"Never mind." Lisa stared at the phone for a moment, then set it back on the receiver. What had happened? Apparently everything hadn't blown over by seventh period. As Lisa returned to her math, her mind was setting up its own problem. Reason-Michelle-got-booted-out + frog-juice-on-Samantha = what-really-happened. Suddenly, Lisa found herself unable to concentrate.

It's over, Lisa told herself. Still, she knew she needed to find something to reassure her of this fact. Journals! That was it. Lisa put aside her math book again, and ran up to her room. She pulled her journals out from the back of the closet.

She was looking for the one from about two months ago, when Michelle had started becoming popular. Instead, she found the one from the beginning of seventh grade. That's when she'd met Michelle and Anne! Lisa turned to another page in it and started reading. Sure enough, there was a passage about the "new girls she'd just met."

Their names are Michelle and Anne. They seem to be really nice, and as equally lost as I am. Hopefully we'll be able to navigate the halls of junior high together, and manage without getting too confused.

Michelle is funny and smart. I first noticed her in Math, when she dropped her books. On the cover of her math book she had drawn a Sierpinski Gasket. We got into a conversation about fractals, but then the bell rang and we had to find our seats.

When I came into lunch, a little bewildered, I had no idea where to sit. Luckily, Michelle saw me and waved me over. I sat down with them, and had a nice lunch. Michelle introduced me to Anne, who I'd met in English.

The entry went on to talk about Anne and the other people at the table, but it didn't even matter that much. Lisa knew what she had to do.

Setting down her journal, she grabbed a backpack and threw into it two skeins of yarn, a couple knitting needles, and some money.

"Mom, I'm going out to Michelle's house!" Lisa shouted as she left her home.

"Have fun, sweetie."

"Will do."

* * *

"I can't remember, do you like Cookie Dough or Triply-Loaded-With-Half-A-Dozen-Things-You-Can't-Even-Taste better?" Lisa asked.

"Triply-Loaded-With-Half-A-Dozen-Things-You-Can't-Even-Taste, all the way," Michelle said, letting Lisa inside. "You came."

"How could I not? We're friends. We've been through some rough patches, and this is just another one of them. Of course I'd come."

"It sure didn't sound that way when you hung up on me."

"I just needed some time to think," Lisa replied, fidgeting with the ice cream. "Now I've thought it through, and I'm here."

"Sorry, I've just been on the defensive. I guess suddenly

realizing that you have no friends does that to you."

"You have friends."

"You're the only one who came over."

"They're still your friends."

"Do you want to sit down?"

"That might be good." Lisa followed Michelle to the kitchen. Lisa pulled a skein of yarn out of her backpack with the needles in it. Michelle gave a hollow laugh.

"You're still not going to convince me to learn how to knit," she said.

"Ah well," Lisa said, putting it back in her bag, "I figured it would be worth a try." She took a spoon from the table and opened up the ice cream. "So," she held out a spoon of the Triply-Loaded-With-Half-A-Dozen-Things-You-Can't-Even-Taste Ice cream. "What happened?"

* * *

"So, let me get this straight," Lisa said. "Samantha insulted us, your friends, and you "accidentally" spilled frog juice on her?" Michelle nodded. "That is amazing. You're my new idol."

"Do you want to know what the best part is?" Michelle asked.

"What?"

"There was a little bit of frog skin left on it. I think she had it

31

on the entire day." Michelle smiled. "And the teacher never even suspected I did it on purpose, because I'm 'Darling, sweet Michelle who never does anything wrong.'"

"Being good certainly does have it's advantages.

The doorbell rang, and Lisa looked at Michelle. "I suggest you go get that."

Michelle looked dubious, but she got up to open the door. She looked slightly surprised to see Anne standing in the doorway.

"Did I miss the ice cream?" Anne asked.

"We just finished it," Lisa replied, gesturing at the pint-sized cartons on the table.

"Darn. So," she tuned to Michelle, "What happened."

Michelle rolled her eyes. "Here we go again." Anne followed Michelle back to the kitchen, where Lisa was waiting. Lisa pulled out her yarn and began to knit.

"I give in," Michelle said. "Lisa, can you teach me how to knit?"

* * *

"So you just continue doing that," Lisa said. "When you're done... Well, tell me then. If I were to teach you now, you might forget by the time that happens."

"Too true," Michelle replied, concentrating on the stitches.

"I should go," Anne said, standing up.

"Me too," Lisa added.

"Thank you," Michelle said, looking directly at them. "Thank you so much for coming by. I don't know what I'd do without you."

"That's what friends are for," Lisa said, giving Michelle an impromptu hug.

"Being around?"

"Exactly. See you in school tomorrow?"

"Of course."

Infinite Monkeys

MEETING BY THE RIVER

by Mike Manolakes

It wasn't fair, James decided. Today was Saturday, it was the first warm day of the year, and he had to spend the afternoon in the university library. He should be out on his bicycle, or playing some tennis, or throwing a Frisbee in the park. But his paper wasn't going to write itself, and if he was going to pass freshman American history, he needed to get his research done. He took another thick book off the stack in front of him and started flipping toward the index.

"James! What are you doing, man?"

James looked up from his book to see Christopher, who lived two doors down on his dormitory floor. Christopher was brilliant but rarely studied; somehow he managed to keep his grade point average up through nothing more than personality and luck. James wished he could be that fortunate. "What does it look like? I've got a paper for History 135 due Wednesday. I may be pulling an all-nighter or two to get it finished on time."

"Too bad." Christopher picked up one of the books James was using, Volume One of a massive three-volume biography. "This looks boring."

"What are you doing here? Don't tell me you're studying."

"No way. Library's got the best vending machines on campus, though, and I had a sudden craving for some gummy worms."

"Delightful. I really do need to work on this paper, Chris --"

"No problem. I can help you with it."

James looked dubious. "Come on, Chris. I don't think I've ever seen you crack a book, unless it's one of your science fiction novels..."

"Alternative history," Christopher corrected him. "I read a lot of alternative history stories. You know, like what if the British hadn't defeated the Spanish Armada, or if the South had won at Gettysburg. I know a lot about history."

"I don't think my professor wants alternative history. She'd rather I stuck to the way events really happened."

Christopher pulled up a chair and planted himself in it. "All right, so let's go over what did really happen. What's your paper about? This guy?" He opened up Volume One to a page near the front, filled with a glossy reproduction of a portrait of a handsome man in a white wig.

"That's right. I'm finding out about what happened in 1780, on the twenty-first of September. There was a meeting by the river..."

* * *

He waited by the edge of the woods, straining his eyes to see if the boat was coming. It was a dark night, without even a hint of moonlight to illuminate the broad Hudson River. And it was quiet: he could hear distant voices from the decks of the British warship, anchored far down the river. But there was another sound, the sound of oars striking and slicing through the water. He searched for the source of the sound, and then he saw it: a small rowboat nearing this side of the river, with four men aboard. Carefully he unshuttered his lantern and approached the riverbank.

"General?" a man whispered from the boat.

"Here, Smith," he answered. "It's safe. Your passenger can disembark."

Once the rowboat had reached shallow water, Smith and the two oarsmen jumped out and pulled the boat onto dry land. Then the fourth man in the boat stepped out. The man's coat looked deep gray in the near-darkness, but even without being able to see its true color, there was no mistaking the uniform of a British Redcoat.

"You're in uniform?" the man on the shore said, surprised.

"They hang spies in this place," the officer answered. "If this turned out to be a trap, I would prefer to be captured in my uniform."

"Of course. Welcome ashore, Major Andre. I'm Benedict Arnold."

John Andre nodded. "We meet at last, sir. I've read your correspondence with great interest. So has General Clinton. Is there a place we can talk? I feel extremely ... exposed here."

"Follow me, Major." To Smith and the oarsmen, Arnold said, "Wait here. The major and I have important matters to discuss, and then you can return the major to his ship."

Benedict Arnold and John Andre walked to the cover of the nearby woods. Arnold walked slowly, his wounded leg bothering him especially this night, and Andre, impatient to get into the cover of the trees, had to force himself to match the slower pace of the American general. When they had at last entered the woods and were far enough within to be completely out of sight, Arnold found a sturdy tree to lean against, taking his weight off his throbbing leg.

Andre waited for Arnold to assume a comfortable position, and then he said, "I deciphered your last letter personally, General. Let me make sure that I did not make any errors in the deciphering. You have agreed to surrender to Sir Henry Clinton's forces the American fortifications at West Point and its garrison. In return, you wish a commission in His Majesty's Army, and the sum of ten thousand pounds in gold. Am I correct?"

"No, sir. The sum was twenty thousand pounds."

"I see. Well, I don't see that the money will be any problem for us. I'll make sure the proper payment is made. Though I confess, I am amused that a man will be too principled to betray his comrades for ten thousand pounds, but he's agreeable to it for twice the sum."

"This is not at all easy for me," Arnold protested. "I do not take this action lightly."

"No, of course not," Andre said. "But consider this -- your action will save the lives of many good men, British and colonial. This rebellion must end eventually, and if our transaction brings that day any closer, than I say it's worth every ha'penny."

"That has been my thought exactly."

The two men stood in silence for a time, and then Major Andre extended his hand. "It's agreed, then?"

Benedict Arnold hesitated, then clasped the British officer's hand. "Yes."

There was another long, awkward pause. Finally Andre said, "You have something for me?"

"Of course." Arnold reached into his coat and brought out several folded documents wrapped in leather. "This is everything you will require. Diagrams of the fortifications, maps of the approaches to West Point, troop emplacements, code signals -- it's all there."

"Excellent." He dropped to one knee and began spreading out the documents on a bed of fallen leaves. "Bring that lantern over here, and show me everything."

For the next several hours, John Andre heard Benedict Arnold explain to him everything the British would need to know to successfully capture and exploit the American fortress at West Point. So immersed were they in the details of the proposed action, it was several minutes before either was aware of a distant low rumbling.

"What's that?" Andre asked.

"It's cannons, I believe."

Both men froze at the sound of hurried footsteps on the fallen leaves that carpeted the forest. It was beginning to get light, and the two men could clearly see the figure of Joshua Smith emerge from the trees in the gray light of dawn. "General Arnold!"

"What is it, Smith?"

"Shore batteries have opened fire on the *Vulture*, sir. She's raised anchor to return downriver."

"I must return to the ship at once!" Andre exclaimed.

Smith shook his head. "It's not safe. The men won't row across the river under fire, sir. It's too late to return you to the *Vulture*."

Andre looked perplexed. "What shall I do?"

Smith looked to Arnold, who nodded. "You'll need to return to your own lines by land, Major. Mister Smith's house is not far from here. We shall go there at once, and we'll dress you in his civilian clothes. I will write you a pass, in the name of 'John Anderson', that will allow you to cross our lines unchallenged. Is that satisfactory?"

Andre looked unhappy, but he said, "I suppose it will have to do. Lead on, Smith."

"This way." Smith took the lantern from General Arnold, and

40

he led the two men swiftly through the woods. Smith seemed unaware of the severity of the wound in Arnold's leg, but the American general did his best to keep up with the villager and the British spymaster. Fortunately, the man's house was not far. Joshua Smith lived in a modest house on the far edge of the woods, where he farmed a small patch of land and kept a few pigs and goats. Once they arrived, Smith led them into the front room of the house, which was dominated by a large stone hearth.

Smith found a plain dark coat for Andre to wear to replace the scarlet uniform coat of a British regular. Andre looked extremely uncomfortable as he removed his own coat to put on Smith's. Once Andre's coat was removed, Arnold could see the dark handle of a large knife in a scabbard that was strapped to the Englishman's belt, but he made no comment.

"This is exactly what I hoped to avoid," Andre said, looking very displeased as he put on the civilian coat.

"An unfortunate necessity." Benedict Arnold sat at a small writing desk and began writing out the pass that would allow Andre to travel unchallenged in territory held by the Continental Army. Andre stood by awkwardly, waiting for the necessary document. Smith, meanwhile, had gone to the stable behind the house to saddle his best horse for John Andre.

Minutes later, the pass was finished, and Andre read the wording carefully. "Will it do?" Arnold asked.

"I hope so, for both our sakes. What is keeping that man with the horse? I wish to depart as soon as possible."

Arnold rose from his chair and walked toward the front door. "Let me find out what the delay is."

But before Arnold could reach for the doorknob, the door opened. Instead of Joshua Smith, there was a short fair-haired man in the uniform of the Continental Army who entered the house. "Hello, General," he said, but his manner was not friendly. He looked grim.

Andre turned pale. "What's the meaning of this, General Arnold?"

"Hello, Colonel Hamilton," Arnold said calmly. "I didn't expect you to come personally."

"Oh, I wouldn't have missed this," the officer said, a note of menace in his voice. "I assume this is Major John Andre, the notorious spy for the King? And out of uniform, no less. So pleased to make your acquaintance. Alexander Hamilton, aide-de-camp to General Washington, at your service."

"I see," Andre said. His voice was heavy with resignation. "So Washington sent you to arrest me?"

"To arrest you, yes, but I wouldn't say that he sent me." It was then that Andre and Arnold became aware of a second figure, standing just a few steps beyond the door's threshold. He approached and stepped into the candle-lit room. The tall man removed his hat and said quietly, "Good morning, Benedict."

"George Washington?" Andre said, astonished.

"I am. For some time I've been reading some remarkable correspondence, Mr. Andre. Your name is mentioned quite prominently in it, sir, as is General Arnold's, and the fortifications at West Point. I understand that a business transaction has been proposed. Correct?"

"I don't understand," Andre said. "How did you see those letters..."

Washington remained silent and nodded in the direction of Benedict Arnold. Arnold himself said nothing in reply.

"You!" Andre exploded. "You've been playing a double game -- pretending to sell out your country, and all the time intending to deliver me to my enemies!"

"Correct," Hamilton said, a smile appearing at last on his handsome face. General Arnold has been kind enough to make copies of his letters to you and General Clinton, and your replies. We have been looking forward with great anticipation to the day when we could place you in custody. That day has arrived."

"I see," Andre said, his rage barely controlled. "So tell me, Mister Benedict Arnold, was there not a drop of sincerity in what you said in those letters? Your disillusionment with the rebels' cause, your disgust at how you had been treated by Congress and your military superiors, your suspicions of the dangers of alliance with the French? Can you deny that you truly did desire to ally yourself with the forces of His Majesty?"

Arnold's voice was barely a whisper. "I cannot deny it. At one time, I did wish to abandon my duty, and give my assistance to the British. It was, as you well know, what my wife wished me to do, and her Loyalist friends as well. When I began our communication, my words were sincere."

"And now?"

"Now, a part of me still regrets that I decided, in the end, to do my duty. I made General Washington aware of what I had done, and placed myself at his mercy. I fully expected to be arrested as a traitor and executed."

"I could not do that," Washington said gravely. "Not to the hero of Fort Ticonderoga, of Quebec, and of Saratoga. Not to a man who had suffered wounds in service to his country. Instead, I gave Benedict Arnold the opportunity to redeem himself."

"He could save his own life by delivering mine?" Andre said. "Not a terribly heroic thing to do, nor much of a trade." He turned to face Arnold. "Benedict, listen to me. It's not too late. You can still be a great man. Your king will reward you richly, with both glory and wealth, if you accept for real the offer that you pretended to accept earlier. If you aid Washington, you'll end up only as an insignificant footnote to a failed rebellion. But join us, and you will be known as the man who saved the British Empire!"

Benedict Arnold hesitated. Up until this moment, he had thought his mind was decided. He would remain true to the cause of the Continentals and give up Andre. But now, hearing the Englishman's words to him, doubt returned to his mind. He opened his mouth to speak, but no words came out. He did not know what to say.

The other three stood looking at Benedict Arnold, each waiting to see what he would do. When it was clear that Arnold was not about to do anything, it was Alexander Hamilton who broke the silence. "Let's go, Major," he said, stepping forward and reaching for Andre's arm.

"No!" Andre exclaimed, and he shoved Hamilton hard with

both hands. Hamilton was thrown violently backward and crashed heavily against the stonework of the hearth, his head making an ugly sound upon impact. He crumpled to the floor and lay still. By this time, Andre had already dashed for the open door of the house and was bolting for freedom.

"Stop him!" General Washington cried, and at once the commanding general rushed out the door, giving chase to the fleeing Englishman. Arnold took a couple steps in that direction as well, but he knew at once it was useless to try to run; his injured leg would not permit it. Instead he turned to look at the fallen form of Alexander Hamilton. Hamilton was unconscious but breathing; blood was dripping slowly from where his head hit the stone hearth. Arnold judged that he would probably survive, so he turned his attention back to Washington's pursuit of Andre.

In the light of dawn, Arnold could make out what was happening far down the dirt road that led to Smith's house. Andre was running hard, but he was not going to escape George Washington, who was an extremely fit and muscular man. Arnold noted that Washington and Hamilton had come without guards or any other soldiers to help them make the arrest; apparently they did not anticipate that it would be difficult for the two of them, with Arnold's help, to place Andre in custody.

As Benedict Arnold limped down the lane to get a closer look, he saw Washington make a leap with arms extended to try to bring down the fleeing British spy. But at that moment Andre stopped running and turned to face Washington. In his right hand something metallic caught the light of the rising sun. Arnold wanted to cry out a warning, but he knew it would be too late -- already Andre was driving the blade of his knife deep into Washington's abdomen. The two men crashed to the ground, but only one got back up to his feet.

"Arnold!" Andre cried, panting heavily. "It's not too late! We can escape together! We can be aboard the *Vulture* before the colonials even know these two are dead!"

Benedict Arnold shook his head. He reached into his coat and drew forth the pistol that he had loaded and primed hours earlier, before Andre's boat had reached the riverbank. He extended his arm, took careful aim, and squeezed the trigger. The sound of the gunshot shattered the quiet of the early morning.

John Andre looked in amazement at the bloody hole that suddenly appeared in his shirtfront before he fell to the ground, dead.

Arnold rushed to where George Washington had fallen. The general was still alive, but his uniform was drenched in blood. The large hunting knife, also red with blood, had fallen to the ground next to Washington. Arnold tore away at Washington's shirt to reveal the wound, long and jagged. He tried to make a bandage out of his own neckcloth, but he knew the wound was mortal. Still he did what he could to try to save the general's life.

"Benedict..." Washington said. His voice was a raspy whisper.

"Save your strength, General. Don't try to speak."

"I never believed you wanted to betray us. I still do not believe it..."

Joshua Smith came hurrying up to them. "I heard the gunshot," he said. "Is he dead?"

"No, not dead, but he needs a surgeon's care," Arnold told him.

"Hitch your horse up to your wagon, and hurry. Then help me lift the general into the wagon -- we must hurry."

"I can help," came a voice from the direction of the house. Alexander Hamilton was standing there, leaning on the door frame. He seemed dizzy from the blow to the head, but otherwise able to function.

"Thank God you're on your feet," Arnold said. "Come and help me, Colonel -- the general's life is in danger."

* * *

James closed the book. "You know the rest."

"Sure," Christopher said. "Washington died a couple of hours later, before they even reached the surgeon. But Hamilton told everyone what a great hero Benedict Arnold was, and the Continental Congress appointed Arnold to take Washington's place as commander of the Continental Army."

"Right. So Arnold came that close to betraying America -- but instead, he goes on to become one of the greatest Americans ever -- the 'Father of His Country'."

Christopher smiled. "Think of the alternative history story you could write about this. What if Benedict Arnold did sell out his country, and George Washington had lived? Who knows, maybe it would have been Washington, not Arnold, who defeats the British at Yorktown. Washington could have been the one to preside at the Constitutional Convention and see that the Constitution is written, instead of Arnold, who would have been disgraced as a traitor. And maybe, just maybe, it's George Washington who becomes the first president of the United

47

States."

"Instead of Benedict Arnold?" James said. "I don't know if you'll get anyone to believe that fantasy."

"I guess you're right. That is kind of far-fetched. Still, you never know. I've got to get going, James. Don't work too hard."

"Too late." James waved good-bye to his friend, then returned to his research. It would be a long night of work on his term paper, here in the undergraduate library of Benedict Arnold University, in the national capital of Arnold, D.C.

JONAS AND THE AWESOME CHILD

by David E. Dean

So, Doctor, you have come here for a story. That's good because I, Jonas, have one for you. It's the best kind - a true one. I know. I was there when it happened sixty years ago. I was only twelve, but I remember it like it was yesterday.

I came from a poor family. When I was ten I went to live with my mother's great uncle, Zachariah. He and my Aunt Elizabeth were old and had no children. Mother told me she asked my Uncle to teach me a trade and hoped he would adopt me. Since Father's death my mother had worn herself out trying to feed the six of us. I didn't want to go but I knew it would help mother. I not only worked around the house I also watched the goats. It wasn't too hard and my Aunt Elizabeth was a wonderful cook.

Uncle Zachariah took his responsibility seriously. He trained me like fathers did their own sons. I felt pleased by his attention and wanted to become like him. I quickly felt secure living with them, that was until I turned twelve.

I remember the day things started changing. Aunt Elizabeth

started preparing early. The house filled with the smell of the bread baking on the stove and the lentil stew simmering over the fire. My job was to turn the spit with the lamb. I had a lot of time to think while sitting by the coals and turning the simmering meat. I remembered my conversation with my uncle just before he left for the temple in Jerusalem.

"I am old," he said, "and I long for a chance to offer incense in the Holy Place in the temple," he sighed. "But there are so many of us priests. That is why I also became a scribe. It is an honorable profession and I hope you will honor it someday as well." He smiled at me. "We priests from the lesser families only work in the temple one month a year. Every day the supervisor priest draws a name. That man offers the incense that represents our people's prayers to God."

He paused and looked toward Jerusalem. "Once a priest offers the incense he can never do it again. In this way as many priests as possible can perform the ceremony. I have never been chosen." He paused. "Soon my time working in the temple will be over. I may never have the opportunity."

I thought my uncle was going to cry, but instead he patted my head and said, "May the Promised One come and deliver us."

That had been a month ago. Turning the spit I wondered, Did he get his chance to offer the incense?

That afternoon Uncle Zachariah returned home. I was so happy I ran to greet him. He only looked and me and smiled. I wondered what was wrong and why he didn't say anything.

My Aunt made quite a fuss over him so I did not learn what had happened until later when I found the scraps of paper. He had been chosen! And as he offered the incense an angel spoke to him. The angel said that my Aunt was going to have a baby. When Zachariah told the angel this was impossible, the angel said that as proof of his prediction Uncle would not speak again until after the baby was born. So Uncle Zachariah wrote everything out for us.

I was amazed by what he said about the baby! My Aunt Elizabeth was old enough to be my grandmother's mother! I wondered if my Uncle was coming down with a fever. You can imagine my surprise when Aunt Elizabeth became pregnant and stopped going to the well for water. At first I pouted because that meant more work for me. Then she told me that the midwife said she needed to rest until the baby was born. I became her errand boy. Everywhere I went people shook their heads in wonder when they asked how my Aunt was.

No more tending the goats! I had to stay near my Aunt to help her. That's how I know what happened next. Almost five months after Uncle Zachariah had seen the angel, someone came to the door. Aunt Elizabeth asked me to see who it was. So I met Mary, my Aunt's cousin, who had arrived unexpectedly.

When Mary told my Aunt how happy she was to see her, Aunt Elizabeth smiled in a funny way and said "Oh, my!" She cradled her stomach with her arms. Then she embraced Mary and asked, "Why should the mother of my Master come into my house."

"How do you know?" Mary asked

My Aunt replied, "My child told me. The moment you greeted me, my baby leaped inside me!"

Mary said, "The Lord God has again visited his people. Let me sing for you." Mary's lilting voice was beautiful and the song full of hope.

I had doubted Uncle Zachariah's message that Aunt Elizabeth was going to have a baby but I was more skeptical over this news, especially when I learned more. You see, I was quite a curious boy. There was a spot on the roof of the house where if I stood just right I could hear everything people said in the room below. I left the two of them alone and that's where I went.

I heard Mary tell Aunt Elizabeth how the Angel, Gabriel, had visited with her. He said that she was blessed by God and would have a baby. Mary had protested that she had never been with a man, but the Angel assured her that God himself would perform a miracle. She would indeed be the mother of God's son, our hoped for chosen one. The baby would save our people from oppression.

I knew something like that just couldn't happen! But then Aunt Elizabeth couldn't have a baby either.

Then Aunt Elizabeth called for me. We needed more water from the well and I stayed busy for the rest of that day. Still Mary was nice to have. She helped a lot with the work in the house. I appreciated that. She stayed for almost three months, but returned home before Aunt Elizabeth had the baby. I didn't want her to go, but she left for Nazareth anyway.

I'd heard the village women talk about her. They said she should go away, that she wasn't wanted in our village and that she should be ashamed of herself. Some even said that if our leaders could enforce the laws Moses wrote they could keep things like this from happening. After Mary left it didn't take long for the women to find something else to talk about.

On the day Mary left my Aunt told me to get a food basket for Mary. I had just handed it to her when Aunt Elizabeth came into the room. She assured Mary that she would always be welcome here in Bethany if things did not go well.

Because of all that happened I almost forgot about Mary. Right after little John was born Uncle Zachariah began talking again. Everyone in town came to see him. People said that God was again speaking to our people and that maybe a prophet had been born.

Our household became very busy. As you can imagine I had a lot more to do. But my Aunt and Uncle had not forgotten Mary. Once I found the two of them watching the baby sleep. My Aunt said that she worried for Mary and hoped everything was well with her. Uncle assured her that Joseph was a good man who would do the right thing.

A few days later we heard lots of news in one day. First, a relative brought a letter from Nazareth. I made sure I was tending the fire when Uncle Zachariah read it aloud to my Aunt. Mary wrote that God had been with her. Joseph had first told her he was going to break the engagement privately to disgrace her no further. But the next day he came back and said that an angel had spoken to him in a dream. They had married and so Joseph claimed the child as his own.

When I said, "Oh!" my Uncle gave me "the look" and I left the room.

I went outside and climbed my favorite tree. From that perch I had the best view in the whole village when the herald accompanied by four Roman horsemen stopped in the village square. He read the mandate from the Emperor Caesar Augustus.

Everyone had to go to their hometowns to register for the tax rolls. Oh, great, I thought, that will be more work for me! That's how I thought when I was twelve.

Bethany was Uncle Zachariah's hometown, so he didn't have to travel. But my Aunt was concerned about her cousin. By now Mary was very pregnant and it was a long trip from Nazareth to Joseph's hometown of Bethlehem.

As the time for the registration got closer, a lot of people we knew left town and many others traveled through our village. It took much longer for me to go places. Aunt Elizabeth said it was because I talked a lot and listened more. About the only good thing about the time was that many of our women relatives from all around Judea and Galilee had come for the registration. That also meant we men (that's what Uncle Zachariah called us) needed to get away. So I got to go with Zachariah into Jerusalem to visit a scholar friend.

I carried some parchments in a pack with some food. The water skin weighed me down the most. Once we got to his friend's house there was nothing for me to do but listen to the old men talk. They started out discussing the teachers who had come from the eastern desert the day before. Their announcement that they were looking for a new King caused a lot of commotion. Then Uncle said they had more important things to do. So he and his friend debated what different teachers taught about the books Moses had written. I tried to follow their discussion the air was still and I was tired from the walk.

A pounding on the door woke me. A servant opened the door and one of King Herod's personal guards stood there. He announced that Herod had ordered all the scholars to come at once. When Uncle Zachariah looked at me my heart sank. I was sure he was going to tell me I had to stay behind. Instead he winked and motioned for me to join him. He placed his hand on my shoulder, "to steady myself" he muttered. His friend looked at my surprised expression, shook his head and smiled.

So I got to see Herod the Great and his palace. It was wonderful, but Zachariah said "don't touch anything." His grip was strong for an old man. I never left his side.

Even I knew King Herod wasn't very religious, so when he asked the scholars where the chosen one of God was to be born the scholars murmured in surprise. With pride and a hint of condescension the scholars answered together quoting from one of our sacred books, "In Bethlehem in the province of Judea, you are in no way the smallest among the leaders because out of you will come a ruler who will guide my people as a shepherd guides his sheep."

Without so much as a "thank you" Herod left the room. We returned to the teacher's house to get our things. Even though it was almost dark, Uncle Zachariah insisted we eat quickly and be on our way. He said, "Jonas, I am uneasy about these events. Many strange things are happening. I should be home with your Aunt and the baby." I did not answer, but just kept my pace steady as my load seemed heavier with each step.

We walked without talking, but gradually I heard a noise behind me. It had gotten dark now as twilight was almost passed. What an unusual time for a caravan to travel! We stepped off the road to let them pass. Even in the dimness it was a wondrous sight. I knew these must be the teachers from the east. I had never seen such fine saddles on camels before. They must be rich too, I thought.

"Greetings, father," one of the men called to my Uncle.

"Greetings to you," he responded.

"We are going to Bethlehem," the man continued. "Our mission is most urgent. Light fails and we are in need of a guide. Do you know anyone who could show us the way?"

I don't know what made me speak. But I heard myself speaking. "I can show you the way. I grew up in Bethlehem. It's only a few more miles." I felt my Uncle's hand tremble on my shoulder.

The man looked from me to Uncle Zachariah before speaking, "Father, even in the east we have read the writings of Moses and honor him. I assure you we will keep him safe and even reward him for his service."

My Uncle bowed and responded, "First permit him to help me home. It is not far. We can travel together."

The man dismounted to walk beside my Uncle. They talked quietly until we arrived home. I was surprised to see my Aunt come to the door. She was holding John as she welcomed us. The teacher complimented her on her healthy grandchild. Even in the dim light coming from the doorway I could see her blush as she responded, "Not my grandchild, my firstborn."

My Uncle brought me a cloak and I mounted the camel with the teacher.

There was so much I wanted to ask this strangely dressed man but I said nothing until he spoke. "I am Gaspar. What is your name?" So our conversation began. He asked about Aunt

Elizabeth, her baby and Bethlehem. He introduced me to the others and I asked him what had brought them all this way. Gaspar said, "Look up." I did and saw the brightest star I had ever seen. "See how it moves." I gazed intently. It did seem to be going before us. "We saw this star when we were in the east and have followed it. We have come to worship the new king of the Jewish people."

I understood what my Uncle meant about strange things happening. Soon I began nodding from the warmth of the cloak and the rocking of the camel. I yawned and shook myself to stay awake. I told Gaspar that even though the star was bright, I needed to walk by the camel to guide it over the road. So down I went. Walking in the brisk night air beside the camel helped me stay awake.

As we traveled I kept glancing up at the star. The closer we got to Bethlehem the less the star seemed to move. Finally it stopped when we arrived outside the main gate to the city. By then it was very dark by then and there were few lights in the town.

"There won't be any room in the town," I said, "not with the registration for taxes. Besides it's too late. You will have to make camp out here."

Gaspar said something in a language I didn't understand and the caravan stopped. Servants started unpacking the camels and someone lit a fire. Gaspar told me that they needed to make some final preparations and I was welcome to dine with them. When he saw my hesitation, he responded by telling me they would have a simple meal of bread and some dried fruit. I squatted by the fire and waited until I noticed some men were coming out of the city gate. Who could be up at this time of night? I wondered.

I walked toward them. "Is that you, Jonas?" One of them asked, and immediately I recognized my friend Eliab's voice. When I was nine we had shepherded his father's flock of sheep.

"Shouldn't you be with the sheep?" I responded, surprised, "Suppose your father finds out!"

"Don't worry young man," a man spoke. "I know he left the flock. We all did. We have seen a wonder."

In the light of the star I could see Eliab's father look first toward the hills south of Bethlehem and then back toward the city. The others had joined us and murmured their agreement.

"We were in the fields." He pointed south. "The sheep were restless and we had a hard time settling them for the night. I was sitting by the fire. Joab quietly played his flute."

I remembered those quiet times when I had been with the sheep at night.

An older man leaned closer to me. In a whisper continued, "Then suddenly a man stood before us. Joab dropped his flute. I reached for my staff. Eliab already had his sling ready when the man said 'Don't be afraid.' His clothes turned white and glowed like hot coals. He seemed to grow bigger as he continued talking. 'I bring you exciting news of great happiness to all the people of the world. Today, this very night a Deliverer has been born in King David's home town. He is the special anointed one of God. This is the sign by which you will recognize the child. You will find him wrapped in strips of cloths, a newborn baby lying in a manger.'"

"Then," Eliab picked up the story, "they were everywhere. A

huge choir of glowing heavenly angels joined the man. They sang praises to God and promised us peace."

"We were speechless," another shepherd spoke up. "Then they were gone. A crowd of shining angels were standing in front of us one moment. Then darkness and quiet the next. I don't know who spoke next but someone said that we should go into the Bethlehem and see this wonderful child."

"So we left the sheep and hurried down the hills." Eliab's father again spoke for the group. "It was then we noticed how bright the star had become." The shepherds looked up. "We had no trouble getting down here. The city was quiet as we went straight to the inn. With all the visitors for the registration we thought that would be the place to start looking for a baby in a manger. Sure enough we surprised the new parents when we asked to see their baby.

"The man asked why we had come," Eliab's father continued, "I said an angel told us to come because the Chosen One of God, the Deliverer, had been born and we would find him lying in a manger. When I spoke of the angel, I saw the father glance at the mother and they both smiled." He paused a moment.

"They let us look at the baby. We knelt before the child. Joab started and soon we were all quietly singing the song of the angel choir. The young mother held the baby close and started to cry. 'Thank you,' she whispered."

"Who were they?" I asked.

Eliab answered, "Joseph and his wife, Mary. They travelled all the way from Nazareth for the registration. Because she was so close to having the baby they couldn't travel quickly. They arrived late and all the guest rooms were gone. They just made it into the town before the baby was born."

"Thank you," I jumped at the voice behind me. Gaspar and the other teachers had approached while the shepherds had told their story. "We have come to see this child." He turned to his companions and asked, "What kind of child is this if his birth is announced in this way?" Gaspar and the others bowed reverently to the shepherds.

"Here," Melchior, one of teachers, offered the shepherds a large cake of dried figs and three round loaves of bread, "Something to eat on your way back to your flocks."

The shepherds accepted the food. After they left my stomach growled. Gaspar laughed as he handed me a small bag with some food in it. I devoured a couple dates and tied the pouch to my belt before hurrying after the teachers.

The inn was at the center of Bethlehem. The stable door was shut when we arrived and knocked. The voice of a weary man asked who was there. I pushed the door open and so saw the full surprise on the faces of Mary and Joseph when the teachers in their fine clothes entered the stable.

Joseph bowed to the visitors with respect and said, "Welcome, but I am afraid I have nothing in the way of hospitality to offer."

"There is none needed," Gaspar spoke for his friends, "We have come a great distance from the east following the star to seek and honor the baby King of the Jews." He knelt as Mary raised the baby from her lap so the men could see. "His name is Jesus," she told them, "He will rescue his people from the wrongs they have done."

"Long have we waited for this day," Gaspar spoke, "We feared we might never see it."

The others knelt with him. They thanked God that the Promised One had finally arrived. Gaspar opened a small chest and set it beside the manger. "Accept this gift as a token of all that is due you." My mouth dropped open at that moment. The box was full of gold coins. Never before, or since for that matter, have I ever seen that much gold in one place!

Melchior set a large pot beside the box. It was full of reddish-brown stones. It didn't know what it was at the time, but I knew from the decorations on the pot it must be valuable. Since then I've learned the contents was myrrh, a vital ingredient for our ceremonial anointing oil and incense.

Next Balthazar placed a tall metal jar beside the box and bowl. He opened it. A powerful fragrance filled the stable. I knew at once it was frankincense. We burn it to cover up really bad smells and I knew it was as precious as gold.

I could hardly take my eyes off the treasures but the baby moved at that time. I looked up to see the confused wonder on the faces of Mary and Joseph. At that moment Mary looked at me and smiled. She motioned to her husband and he leaned close to hear her. He nodded and turned to look at me. He came to me as the teachers continued to talk quietly with Mary.

Joseph said, "Mary recognized me and thought you might know who could give us some water or at least some empty pots I fill at the well.

"My mother lives down the street. I'll go get some!" Off I ran toward my home.

Did I surprise Mother when I knocked on the door and woke her up! She stated muttering about what she was going to tell old Jedediah, the innkeeper, when she heard he had turned away a pregnant woman ready to give birth. She grabbed some clean cloths and a large jar of water and sent me with two empty buckets to the well. I stopped at the well as she hurried to the stable.

Soon Joseph soon joined me. He said, "The women sent me away to help you." We finished quickly and returned to the stable. Mary looked refreshed but was nodding when we arrived. My mother hushed us and then laid a blanket on some straw near the doorway. She whispered to Joseph, "Jonas will sleep here. If you need anything in the night send him to me."

I was so excited I didn't think I would be able to sleep, but I did almost as soon as I lay down. It was dark outside when I opened my eyes again. I lay there wondering what was different. It wasn't until I went outside I realized what it was. The bright star was gone!

In panic I thought, The teachers! and ran along the street to the city gate. I could hear movement and hushed talking. They were packing up!

"Ah, Jonas," Gaspar said when I arrived. He was carrying a torch and a pouch. "I was coming to find you. You have saved me a walk. We promised to pay you for your services."

How could I have forgotten?

He handed me the cloth pouch that was heavier than it

appeared. I opened it and peered inside. Gaspar held the torch closer so I could see. My mouth opened as I saw some silver coins, one gold coin, a ring and a simple silver drinking cup. I kept a silver coin and gave the rest of the money to my mother. I still have the ring, but I gave away the drinking cup a long time ago.

After looking into the bag I asked Gaspar why they were leaving so quickly. "God has warned us not to return to Jerusalem. We all had the same dream and now need to leave as quickly as we can. We think we can be out of his territory before King Herod realizes we are not coming back. Thank you, Jonas, for all your help." He paused and looked at the stars, "God has shown us such wonders. You, I think" he put his hand on my shoulder, "have seen your share." With that he turned and mounted his camel.

I stood watching until even the sound of their caravan ceased. I found myself alone with the noises of the late night. I shook my head and carried my sack back into the town. I needed to put it someplace safe before anyone saw me with it. I went home; Mother was up early preparing the morning meal so I went into my old room and hid the sack in my secret spot under the bed.

I don't know how my mother knew I was there but she called me. "Take this food to Mary and Joseph." I grabbed the bundle and ran back to the stable.

To my surprise Joseph was loading the donkey. I must have looked confused because Joseph told me that the same angel he had seen in Nazareth had talked to him in a dream. This time he had told Joseph leave Bethlehem and go to Egypt.

"Then you must go quickly." I told him, "The teachers have

already left. God warned them in their dreams last night. They won't tell King Herod about the baby."

Joseph looked so tired at that moment, and when I said, "I know a little used path out the south gate," Joseph looked relieved.

Mary handed me the baby. I held my breath. I couldn't believe that I was holding God's Chosen One in my arms. He was such a small baby wrapped tightly in the strips of cloths, but he was awake I'm sure he look me straight in the eyes and smiled.

Joseph helped Mary onto the donkey before taking the baby from my arms. "This way," I said and we left the stable. Fortunately the sky had not yet started to lighten so there weren't many people about. We quietly left Bethlehem and without difficulty found the path leading up the hill off the main road. In an hour we passed through the olive groves and beside some vineyards before climbing a fairly steep hill to the crest of the ridge. As we started down the other side, I thought I heard trumpets but wasn't sure until later.

We walked without talking. I lead the donkey and Joseph walked to one side. He seemed quite protective of Mary and the Baby. Well after sunrise the path we followed joined a road.

"This road goes down to the Great Sea." I pointed the way, "Follow it until it meets the coastal highway. Then go south to Egypt."

"Thank you Jonas," Mary spoke, "You were a gift to us as precious as any the teachers gave."

I stepped back and shook my head in disbelief.

"Yes, young Jonas," Joseph stepped before me and put his hands on my shoulders, "I am sure God has good things in store for you. Now may God bless you and keep you safe. May He smile upon your way and give you peace."

Mary held the baby up so I could see Jesus again.

Then I stood there and for the second time that morning watched someone leave me behind. Even as a twelve year old boy I knew I had a part in these awesome events. Little did I know it would be almost thirty years before I again saw Jesus.

But that, my friend, is another story for another time.

Infinite Monkeys

THEN BUT FOR YOU GO I

by Tim Yao

"I saw a man walking by the sea,
Alone with the tide was he.
I looked and I thought as I watched him go by:
There but for you go I"
- Alan Jay Lerner (Brigadoon)

John Isel hung up the phone and stared with disbelief at his calendar--today (today!) was his anniversary and he had forgotten to buy his wife a gift. Worse, she had been hinting for months what it was she wanted--tickets for the local revival of the Lerner and Lowe musical Brigadoon--and now it was sold out. If only he had remembered even a week earlier (or so the clerk had apologetically told him), he could have gotten tickets for tonight. But no, his attention, his passion, had been wrapped up in his secret project, the one that would finally earn him the acclaim he deserved. Even his best friend Marty, who was also his research partner and boss, had laughed at his ideas! John's hands clenched at the memory.

Now, though, maybe his work would pay off and he could save his anniversary celebration at one swoop... John eyed his contraption warily. It occupied the left corner of his messy desk, an amalgamation of parts from Radio Shack. He grinned wanly but with some pride at what he, the neurologist and electronics hobbyist, had managed to build. At the office, Marty's self-named Bristoltron had cost several million dollars and occupied most of a large lab; here, John had spent less than two hundred dollars for a machine that would do more than enhance memories. Here, with the Iseltron, John would make history by literally remaking history!

John fretted a little at the thought of this first application. There was some risk in what he would be trying; the Iseltron would be modifying, in precise fashion, specific portions of his brain chemistry. Was getting tickets for his wife a worthy objective?

John sighed and placed the modified headphones on his head, over his temples. They had been on sale for under $15 at Radio Shack; a part of him wished for the sleek custom helmet that Marty had ordred for the Bristoltron. Still, there was something to be said for being thrifty.

Carefully, he precisely aligned the dial, watching the readout on the LCD display that monitored the relatively tiny voltage that fed into the heart of his device. The jury rigged circuit board in the spare external drive case held not one but two tiny special integrated chips he had purloined from the store of spares that Marty kept at work.

John frowned for a moment, blushing guiltily; but it wasn't as though Marty realized just precisely what those IC's were capable of. And there were so many spares and other parts--John knew Marty'd never miss them.

Drawing a deep breath, John set the dial for two weeks prior (best to play it safe, he thought) and then, hand shaking, pushed the red toggle forward...

The now familiar grey numbness ate away at his consciousness, but faster and with greater intensity than his earlier experiments had invoked when he had sent his memories back a couple hours.

John blinked and felt a momentary wave of vertigo.

Instead of sitting at his desk, he was in a moving vehicle.

In fact, he was driving it, both hands on the wheel. It took only a small movement to correct the swerve. John ran the fingers of one hand lightly over the Chevy's old steering wheel.

"Oh John!" Hannah gushed, sounding astonished. "You *did* remember!"

He smiled, eyes on the road, but lit with triumph. John's mind began to spin, thinking how his invention might gain him sufficient funds to replace the old car. "Of course, dear!" he replied. "I had it in my mind all along." He grinned.

She leaned in to him and kissed him again, no easy feat with both of them wearing seatbelts in the old Chevy. John breathed in the clean scent of her, feeling a stray lock of her dark red hair brush against his cheek.

Indeed, his own memories were a little fuzzy now. He dimly remembered pushing the switch in the then future; and, two weeks ago, he vividly recalled the sudden mental prod to buy tickets for Brigadoon. The next two weeks had passed in a blur until today, when the memory of his experiment had resurfaced.

Suddenly the engine coughed. John looked down at the display. Empty! He cursed. What a way to end what had been a wonderful evening. As the engine died, he managed to pull over to the side of the road.

Stuck in an inner city neighborhood in the dark and late at night. John frowned.

"Don't worry, dear," Hannah said. "I'll just call AAA." And she fished around in her tiny evening purse. "That's funny, I thought I had brought the cell phone along..."

John, who had always thought cell phones were an unnecessary and intrusive luxury, suddenly felt true regret. "It's ok, Hannah," he said. "You just stay here and I'll go find a phone or a service station."

"John, I.. I don't think I want to stay here in the dark without you." She looked at the deserted street and shivered. John thought for a moment and then nodded.

"Ok," he said. "Let's go together." John locked the doors to the car, then took Hannah's hand. She held his hand tightly as they made their way down the street.

A car drove up beside them. A man wearing jeans, a dark jacket and a handkerchief on his head got out. "Can I help you two?" he asked.

"Yes, please!" John said. "We're stuck with no gas and no cell phone. Can you help take us to a gas station?"

The man turned away and reached behind him, bringing forth a small, dark object. As he stepped forward, John saw the light from the street lamp glimmer off of the barrel of a gun. The man's eyes were bloodshot, his expression strained as his gaze darted nervously around the shadows. Sweat gleamed on his cheeks and dripped from his nose.

John froze, petrified. Hannah took a cautious step forward. "What do you want?" she asked, with only a small quiver in her voice.

"Your money!" The man's gun hand shook.

A dog barked loudly. The man started and a shot rang out, impossibly loud. The man stared stupidly at the gun in his hand. Hannah staggered back and then fell. John reached for her but could only slow her fall, not stop it. He knelt by her, dimly aware of the man running away.

Something hot and wet covered his hands.

Hannah opened her mouth, her breath loud and ragged. No words came forth. She shuddered, then fell still in his arms.

Hands trembling, checked her pulse. Nothing. He began administering CPR, sobbing.

Tears still were running down his cheeks some fifteen minutes later when the police arrived. His arms ached and his hands shook from the attempted CPR.

The ambulance arrived minutes later; but it was too late.

John could not stop weeping. His life, everything he had

worked for: gone in an instant. One of the policemen guided him to the Chevy and drove him home, followed by his partner in the squad car.

Half an hour later, he was fumbling with the front door keys. The policeman had to help him.

"Good night, sir."

John closed the door, alone in the foyer, horribly alone in his house.

Out of habit, he went into his home office and sat down at his desk. The device, the Iseltron, gleamed in the light of the old desk lamp. Bitterly, John glared at the machine. If not for his fiddling with time for those stupid tickets, his darling wife would still be alive...

Tears ran silently down his cheeks. And yet...

John picked up the modified headset. His breathing quickened and his eyes narrowed. The Iseltron was a time machine. Maybe there was a way he could save Hannah...

He found an envelope and picked up a ballpoint pen. Brigadoon had started at 8 pm; he and Hannah had departed the theater around 10 pm. It was now 1:43 AM in the morning.

How far back should he go? What action of his would he need to change? Hands trembling, John put down the pen without writing anything. He rubbed his eyes, feeling physically, mentally and emotionally drained and exhausted.

He had an effective time machine. It wouldn't help Hannah for him to make the wrong decision now; and he wouldn't lose anything by waiting till the morning when he was thinking more clearly...

John rose from his desk, but the ache in his heart and the realization that Hannah was gone made him turn around and sit down again. He would just need to ensure that the Chevy had enough gas--then there would be no need to stop after the show in that bad part of town and everything would be alright...

He thought back on the day. If he and Hannah left a little early for the show, they could stop by their neighborhood gas station... Six hours earlier ought to do it, he thought.

Carefully, he placed the headphones on his head and pushed the lever forward...

* * *

"... and if we don't leave soon, we'll be late for the show," Hannah said, tugging on his arm.

"Hannah!" John exclaimed and he took her in his arms and planted a long, passionate kiss.

Hannah kissed him back and then said, "Come on, John. Keep your mind on the show..." She led him over to the car. "Go sit down, dear."

"Of course," John said. "Let's just stop for gas before we go..." He checked his watch, an old but serviceable Seiko. It was already after 7:30 pm! How had he miscalculated? Or had the Iseltron's calibration been faulty? He frowned. His earlier foray hadn't been so time-dependent... the calibration had been based on earlier, much shorter "trips". Maybe the scale wasn't linear...

"Gas!" Hannah exclaimed, getting in her side and peering at the meter. "It looks like there's enough gas to get us there and back..."

John looked at the meter. It was at least half full. He frowned. "Uh, ok..." he said. Inwardly, his memories of the horrifying day were already beginning to fade.

"I wonder if anyone is siphoning our gas..." he muttered.

"Don't get all paranoid on me," Hannah said.

John sighed and then pulled out from the driveway.

They drove on in silence.

"You know, John," Hannah said. "I once played a role in a community theatre production of Brigadoon. I was in high school at the time..."

"That's nice, dear," John replied automatically, his mind focused on the Iseltron. From his theory about how it worked, the "distance" the signals had to travel along the "pink worm" that humans formed in four dimensional space-time should be linear. And he had performed several calibrating tests before the first big trip back two weeks...

"...you're a million miles away." Hannah's voice was sad.

"Oh, I'm sorry, Hannah," John replied. "Uh, just caught up in a technical problem."

There was a long pause. Then Hannah said in a small voice, "I thought tonight was supposed to be for us to spend some time together..."

John turned to look at her. Hannah hadn't changed much over their years together. She still wore her honey blond hair at shoulder length; and her face was achingly beautiful. She looked very sad.

Blam!

"Oh, damn!" John exclaimed as the car jerked. He slammed on the brakes. Fortunately, no one was following them closely.

He knew from the sound and the feel of the car that they had a flat tire.

"I'm so sorry, Hannah," he said, getting out of the car. He took off his jacket and rolled up his sleeves and then walked over to open the trunk...

* * *

By the time that he had changed the tire, it was almost 8:30 pm. Hannah hadn't said a word to him as he slid back into the driver's seat. The engine coughed as he started the car. John forced himself not to grip the steering wheel so tightly. He felt grimy and tense. The engine coughed again.

John frowned and knocked on the gas gauge with his knuckle. To his horror, the gauge flickered and reset itself. It was near empty. He cursed.

"We're almost out of gas," he said grimly. "The gas gauge was wrong before."

Hannah sighed and they drove on.

Then she pointed. "Look, John," she said. "A gas station... it must be karma."

They were not in a very good neighborhood, but it was still early in the evening and there were other cars around or at least driving by. John pulled into the gas station, hopped out and began to fill up his car. Hannah opened her own door and stood up, pacing a little. "Don't worry," John called out to her. "We'll still make it to the show before intermission..."

Just then, a man emerged from the gas station Quikmart. The man wore a handkerchief on his head. John's eyes widened in recognition. "Hannah!" he shouted "Get down! That man has a gun!"

The man stared at John, fear and anger on his face. Hands trembling, the man reached behind himself to pull out his gun. He raised it and Hannah, seeing her husband in mortal danger, threw herself at the man. The gun went off and Hannah fell heavily...

* * *

The next few days were a blur. John did not sleep, his mind filled with what-if scenarios.

Marty came by the house with a casserole. "You look terrible, John," he said, putting the casserole into the refrigerator. "Barbara made this for you. She said to heat it at 350 for thirty minutes." He shrugged off his overcoat and slung it over the back of a chair.

"I ... thank you, Marty. Please thank Barbara for me." John ran fingers over the thick unshaven stubble over his jaw. He glanced over at Marty, who was clean cut and neat in his red sweater and dark slacks. John suddenly felt self-conscious in his old t-shirt and sweat pants.

"Say," Marty said over by the desk. "What's this? Something for your aquarium?"

John looked up. "It's my time machine," he said dully. "If I hadn't used it, Hannah would still be alive today."

"Huh?"

"Do you remember when we had that talk? It was about a month ago... We were brainstorming what was happening with that Bristoltron that enhanced memories."

Marty nodded, fiddling with the dials on John's device.

"Well, I followed through with my line of thought; and this was the result."

"I... I confess I don't remember what your line of thought was," Marty looked up from his fiddling to cast a mild blue-eyed gaze at his partner.

John sighed. "You never take my ideas seriously, Marty."

"Sure I do," Marty said. "After all, without our paper on the effects of Bristol rays on enhancing memory, which included many of your ideas, we wouldn't have won that grant or the research prize."

"Well, that paper is flawed, Marty! My theory provides the

77

solution to the problem with yours. There is an element of time, that fourth dimension, in your Bristol rays." When Marty didn't reply, John forged ahead. "Look, with the Bristoltron (and I really dislike that name!) we're able to enhance memories from specific time periods depending on the amount of power we supply, right?"

Marty nodded, but looked skeptical.

John continued. "You thought that we were somehow tuned into different parts of the memory core of the brain, perhaps by exciting different frequencies. My theory... my theory was that your Bristol rays are somehow reaching back along the fourth dimension and retrieving memory states within a person's mind so that they are superimposed upon our current selves."

"You've been reading too much Rob Bryanton," Marty said. "I'm sorry I ever introduced you to that website of his ..."

John pointed at Marty with a trembling hand. "You said that before! But you're wrong. Bryanton's explanation of the ten dimensions is brilliant. Humans, in the fourth dimension, are like a pink worm whose path intersects many points in space and time. The Bristoltron is able to traverse the fourth dimension and influence our brain waves."

"You're the neurologist, not the physicist," Marty said mildly. "But let's say that your theory is correct. What does this ... this high school assemblage of electrical components do?"

John smiled. "That," he said, "is what I call the Iseltron. It improves upon the Bristoltron's design by utilizing my theory. Many simplifications are possible once you do that. And it then takes a snapshot of a person's current brain pattern and superimposes it upon a specific instance in that person's past, simply by varying the power."

"Look!" John said as Marty's face took on the expression of a man whose friend has gone quietly mad. "I know it sounds crazy, but I've used it twice already. I sent my current mind state back two weeks so that I would buy tickets for Brigadoon before they sold out. And ..." John's voice trailed off and he closed his eyes. Hannah!

"Show me," Marty said, getting up from the desk.

"Ok," John said, taking a deep breath before putting the headphones on his temples. He tried to squash the feelings of foolishness. High school project indeed! "Ok, Marty. What do you want me to do?"

"How about if you go back to when I first arrived and you convince me to write a note to myself?"

"Ok." John made the calculations and set the power level.

"No, wait, that won't work..." Marty said.

But John pushed the lever forward...

* * *

Marty came by the house with a casserole. "You look terrible, John," he said, putting the casserole into the refrigerator. "Barbara made this for you. She said to heat it at 350 for 30 minutes."

"I ... thank you, Marty. Please thank Barbara for me."

"Say," Marty said over by the desk. "What's this? Something for your aquarium?"

Suddenly John froze in place for a moment and looked up. He walked over to Marty with a pen and a pad of paper. "Quick!" he said. "Marty, humor me and write a note to yourself!"

"Okay..." Marty said slowly, looking up at his taller friend. He wrote: Dear Marty, my friend is going crazy. Signed, Marty.

"Now what?" Marty asked.

John sighed. "It was a bad experiment. You see, now I have to explain to you about my time machine..."

Five minutes later, he concluded, "So then you suggested I go back in time to ask you to write a note to yourself. So I did and so you did." He handed Marty the note.

"Yes... and I remember writing that note. But that's no proof that your machine works."

John sighed.

"Look, John," Marty said, patting his friend compassionately on the shoulder. "If your machine works the way you say, there is no way you will ever be able to prove it to an external observer. They will always be a part of the world you've remade by essentially traveling back in time. Or, more correctly, sending present day information into the past to yourself."

"I hadn't thought of that," John admitted. He thought for a moment. "Hey, how about if you tell me some information that you have now but that I wouldn't have. I'll go back to before you tell it to me and then that will prove to you that the machine works!"

"I guess that would work," Marty replied. "Ok. Tell my other self that ... that I know you've been taking supplies from work." He looked evenly at John.

John looked away. "I... I'm sorry, Marty. I was planning to return all of it... eventually."

Marty smiled. "Hell, it's ok, John. If I really cared, I would have said something to you about it." He chuckled. "Think of it as my answer to HP's policy of encouraging innovation from their employees."

John, feeling relieved, thanked Marty.

"Ok. Let's do this experiment." John adjusted the dials to ten minutes and pushed the lever forward...

Nothing happened.

"Something wrong?" Marty asked.

"Uh, no, I don't think so," John said. He turned the dials back another half hour.

* * *

"Hi, Marty," John said. "Thank you for coming by. Please thank Barbara for the casserole."

Marty gave him an amused look. "How did you know I was coming over? Did Barbara call you?"

John shook his head. "No... I'll have to show you this. But first, let's stick that casserole in the oven for thirty minutes at 350..."

Marty took his coat off. "John, I confess I thought you'd be a wreck after what you've been through. But you seem ... ah... very purposeful."

"That's because of your help, Marty." John brought his friend into the den and went through the explanation.

"... and then you said that you forgave me and that this was your way of encouraging employee innovation."

Marty shook his head. "I am amazed by all of this, John." His eyes narrowed. "If I were the suspicious type, I would think that this whole invention was a way to get out of trouble with me."

John said nothing.

"But it is true that I knew about your thefts from the office and that I was deliberately looking the other way. Ok, let's say that your theory is correct. What will you do now?"

John's eyes lit up, though he didn't smile.

"This machine still can save Hannah. I just have to go back to a little earlier on the day of the show and make sure my gas tank is full and that I keep my eyes on the road..."

"Sure!" Marty said. "While you do that, let me go check on the casserole. You look like you haven't eaten since ... for days." He headed to the kitchen.

"Marty?" John called out.

"Just a moment," Marty called from the kitchen.

John changed the dials slightly. He would insist they stop at a gasoline station near their home this time... He pushed the lever forward. Nothing happened. John cursed.

"What's wrong?" Marty asked, walking into the study.

"It didn't work this time," John said. "My attempt to revise history failed; I was going to go back a third time, but something's not working."

"Maybe you've blown a circuit?" Marty suggested. He rummaged around the desk to come up with a circuit tester. Half an hour later, they both sat back, puzzled. "Your circuits look fine," Marty said. "I wonder if the problem isn't hardware based but theoretical..."

"What do you mean, Marty?"

"Well, you were just trying to send your thoughts back to a time slot that you had already sent your thoughts back to... Think of it like a conveyor belt with candy on it, like in that I Love Lucy show. There are many candies arranged in different patterns. You now have the ability to go back in time a ways to rearrange the candies. But if you try to do it again, you not only have the candies at that spot in time on the conveyor belt, you have your own hands there arranging the candies to a specific pattern. Maybe your machine is unable to rearrange the neuron states a second time because your machine is already rearranging them then at that time."

"But I was able to go back twice within your visit..." John frowned. "No, it failed the first time--I had to go back further the second time."

Marty rubbed his chin. "Maybe the size of the window in which you can send your memories is related to how far back in time you send them. That is, shorter trips have smaller windows; longer trips have longer windows of exclusivity..."

John nodded.

"...but that doesn't mean that you can't change that history... it just means you have to go further back in time to a spot you haven't visited and change things then." Marty snorted. "Good God! Now I sound as crazy as you do!"

John thought aloud, pacing. "I can't go back to undo the purchase of the tickets; I can't change the trip to the show or the trip to the gas station..."

"Hey," Marty said. "I have an idea! What if you look up the winning lottery ticket number for before you buy the tickets? You win the lottery and then instead of taking Hannah to the show, you can take her on a cruise!"

"I only have three vacation days left this year," John said...

"Hey, as your boss, I hereby approve you to take some vacation under the table. After all, you've been putting in a lot of time..."

"Marty," John said. "If I go back and do that, you won't have approved the vacation."

"John," Marty said. "If you win the lottery, you won't have to work anymore anyway!"

The two fired up John's aging PC and looked up the winning lottery number.

"How is your number memory retention?" Marty asked.

Two days later, they had drilled the winning lottery number into John's mind so thoroughly that he remembered it better than he did his own social security number.

"Hey John," Marty said. "If this works, can you give me some of the winnings?"

"Sure, why the hell not," John said. "After all, my primary mission is to save Hannah!"

"Yeah," Marty said, with enough good taste to look abashed.

John set the dials and pushed the lever forward...

* * *

John looked around. He was sitting at his desk. The desk calendar showed he had sent his thoughts back just two days before he would buy the Brigadoon tickets... He looked at the clock and swore. It was 4:45 PM. The deadline for buying the lottery tickets was 5 PM. He ran to the back door, almost knocking down Hannah, who was walking into the house with an armful of groceries.

"Hannah!" he shouted and swept her into his arms, giving her a big kiss. Her groceries fell to the floor.

She pushed him back. "John! Now look what you've done!" She bent down to pick up the groceries. "And you smashed the eggs!"

John looked at his watch. It was now ten till! "Hannah," he said. "I've got to go to the grocery store. I... I can't explain it."

"John! I just came from there. Now be a good boy and help me unload the groceries..."

The lottery numbers filled his mind.

"I love you, Hannah!" he called out and then turned to run for the car, not even stopping to close the trunk.

Minutes later, he pulled into the handicap parking spot, the only one close to the door. Ignoring the hostile stares of the other shoppers, he glanced at his watch. Three minutes to 5 PM!

He ran inside, grabbed a handful of lottery forms, filled one out in record time and then shoved it at the teenager clerk.

"Come on!" he yelled. "Punch it in!"

The teenager picked his nose as he processed the ticket.

"Sorry sir," he said. "You just missed the deadline."

* * *

John groaned as he removed the headphones from his head. Marty was sitting beside him.

"Did it fail again?" Marty asked. John shook his head.

"I missed the filing deadline," John said. Then he stood up, picked up the whole machine and threw it against his wall of books. It fell into a number of pieces. He put his head in his hands and cried.

Marty put his hand on his friend's shoulder.

"We can save her," he said. "We can save Hannah."

John looked up.

"There is one tried and true way to do it... but we'll need to rebuild your machine."

Moments later, they were headed off to the neighborhood Radio Shack.

Half an hour later, as they walked into the house, they smelled the wonderful smell of Barbara's lasagna. "Just in time," Marty said, smiling. He went off to the kitchen to turn off the oven and pull the lasagna out.

After dinner, they methodically put together the machine. "We have to calibrate it against my lifespan," John said. "For some reason, the Iseltron can only look backwards in time. There is only one time axis."

Marty mused. "Maybe that is a sign that the theory of an infinite number of parallel universes is true... You can look backwards because your history is set. But you cannot look forwards because your future is yet undetermined." He sighed and patted the machine. "Maybe someday..."

"You're a good friend, Marty," John said.

"Hell," Marty said. "You invented it once; maybe you'll invent it again someday..."

John carefully adjusted the dials. He looked heavenward and said, "I'm coming to you, Hannah!" and pushed the lever forward...

* * *

"May I help you sir?" A teenager in a red Radio Shack vest stood before him. "Anything you need help finding?"

John stood there, his sheaf of notes and circuit designs held trembling in one hand. He took one long, lingering look at them and then looked up at the kid. "No," he said softly. "Not this time around." He tore the notes in half and then in half again.

He sighed, smiled wistfully and dropped the notes in the trash and left the store without looking back.

* * *

"Say," said Marty. "Don't you and Hannah have a big night planned for tonight?"

"Yes," John said, smiling. "Dinner at The Chalet and then Brigadoon downtown. I've been planning for our anniversary for weeks."

"Well, you definitely deserve a night off. You've been putting in so much time on our work." Marty shook his head. "I confess I didn't think you had it in you. But the improvements you've introduced to the Bristoltron have been fantastic! We're getting a lot of interest from outside investors. Well worth that advance bonus."

John looked up at Marty, "I'm just glad to be able to contribute to our company's bottom line. And," he added with a grin, "I have enjoyed driving our new VW Passat."

Marty grinned and clapped John's shoulder. "I'm glad to hear it, John. Now scoot! Go prepare for your anniversary celebration. You deserve a wonderful night!"

* * *

Later that night, Hannah rolled over and looked down at John, her honey blond hair falling across his face. "Thank you," she said. "Tonight was simply magical!"

"Happy anniversary, darling." John replied. "You make my life magical." And then words were no longer needed.

Infinite Monkeys

NOT A GOOD FIT

by Timothy Paulson

Ron looked out the window as his son, Nathan, got on the bus at the end of the long drive way. This was Nathan's second week riding the bus to his new school and he was still so excited to get on each day. It was heartwarming to watch. Nathan bounded up the steps of the bus, each one taking his full effort to mount, and looked so small disappearing into the bus as the doors swooshed closed. The boy sat in the first row of the bus and looked out the window waving and smiling brightly as the bus pulled away.

"He's doing so well," he said turning to his wife who was looking out the kitchen window with him, "Ally, I can't believe how long we banged our heads against a brick wall trying to make it work at Ridge Valley. I feel just terrible about how hard we were on him."

"I know I just can't believe how well he has transitioned into kindergarten at Emerson Elementary ."

"It's amazing what a good teacher can do."

"He just needed some discipline and to know what was

91

expected of him… and someone not to let him get away with bad behavior. I get so mad just thinking about it. How they blamed him for what they were putting him through."

"I know. I mean he's not an easy kid by any means but I knew he could not be as bad as they were making him out to be. I can't believe I pushed so hard to keep him at that school."

Ron thought back to the meeting they had with Nathan's previous kindergarten teacher, Miss Lacy, and the Director of Ridge Valley, Miss Julie, just before Christmas break. Ally had said going in that she was concerned that they were going to kick Nathan out of school at the meeting. But he had refused to believe it. He agreed that there had been a few calls home about hitting and throwing things and a previous meeting about strategies for Miss Lacy to work on with Nathan. But kick him out, it didn't seem like things could possibly have gotten that far without more contact from the school. They had sat down on opposite ends of a table and Miss Lacy had opened up the conversation.

"First let me say some positive things about Nathan and that we really care about his well being. He is smart and loving and very energetic, does well with the works when he's focused. He is a very smart young man and we care about him… well I guess that's it," and she cast a sideways glance at Miss Julie, who just nodded.

"What are you are trying to say," Ally said, although both she and Ron realized exactly what they were trying to say.
"We think that Nathan is not well suited for this classroom."

"Are you kicking him out of the school?"

"Well, no…" Miss Julie addressed them now. "We just think you ought to consider moving him and if there is another incident we will have to ask that you remove him from the school." The Director was a short stout woman with a grating voice, a woman that Ally had grown more and more wary of over the course of the year and half that Miss Julie had been in charge of the school. "It may just be in his best interest to be in a different setting, he may need a more structured environment than the environment that we provide here at Ridge Valley." Ron and Ally did not respond so Miss Julie continued. "I'm not talking about months here but weeks… and if there is another incident he would have to be removed immediately."

"What do you mean by another incident and what do you mean by immediately."

"I mean if he harms another child, if he hits or throws things at anyone again."

"So any day I could get a phone call and then that is it, I have to remove him from the school and find him another situation. We can't live like that waiting for the phone call. How often does this happen that he is harming another student."

"He is a disruptive presence in the school on a daily basis. In a class of 24 kids he is taking up about 2 hours out of the seven hours that I am teaching. We have tried every strategy we can to deal with him and it is just not working out," Miss Lacy interjected back into the conversation.

"A daily basis, you've only reported a couple of instances to us. We've had like two or three incident reports come home. How can you be kicking him out?"

93

Miss Julie shifted uneasily in her chair, "well we sent home the policy on discipline with the last report."

Ron and Ally glanced at each other and he shook his head. When that report had come home with a photocopy of the discipline policy on it Ally had told him that she thought they were preparing to kick Nathan out of school but he had laughed it off. "There is no way that is how they would tell you it must just be a standard attachment so you know the whole process." He should have known enough to trust her instincts when it came to education since she was a teacher herself.

"Listen we are new at this too, we have never gone through this process before," Miss Julie broke the silence that had reached an uncomfortable length.

"Well, grab a pencil, honey, and take some notes, because this is not how you do it. You don't just send a copy of the policy home with no additional comment and then a month later call the parents without telling them what you want to talk about and then tell them you're kicking their son out of school."

The pair on the other side of the table seemed a bit taken aback by Ally's vehemence.

"Well, we are just afraid to turn our back on him, we don't know what to do." Miss Julie said in a voice that was showing strain and defensiveness. "We've tried every possible strategy that has been suggested to us, we met with all the other teachers and no one had any further suggestions."

"We tried the stoplight, the calm down bench, the social stories and nothing consistently worked with him. He can just get out of control and we can't stop him. He does not do his works and we are concerned that he is not getting the education he should and he is interfering with the education of the other children as well. We think he may not be suited for our classroom environment."

"Are you saying that you are giving up on Nathan?" Ally looked from one to the other of the women across the table from her and neither one of them responded. "Make no mistake about it because you are failing him as teachers and as a school. I think that this is learned behavior at this school and he acts the way he does because he thinks he is allowed to. Let me give you an example, from the moment I drop him off he is allowed to be wild and no one has ever stopped him. He jumps out of the car yelling and runs into the building waving his arms about and everyone just laughs and shrugs it off but it sets the tone that he thinks it is acceptable behavior. You want strategies for him? I will give you strategies. I will come into the classroom and observe the class and Nathan's behavior and I will give you the strategies that will work with him."

The discussion had continued for several minutes with them finally agreeing that they would continue to work with Nathan and not kick him out of school and that Ally would come into the classroom to observe the behavior. Ally decided to observe the beginning of the afternoon class and then come back the Monday after the Christmas break and observe for the entire day.

Ally had come home that night fuming about the situation. "I went into the classroom and Miss Lacy was reading to some of the students in a circle, but several of the students were just roaming around the room including Nathan," she reported, "he was just walking around singing to himself and I walked up to him and sat him down in the circle and told him to be quiet. Miss Lacy just looked up at me, shrugged and said 'well we lost few, ha ha' – can you believe that. She just seemed unaware of what was going on in her classroom, this may be worse than I feared.

95

Also, I talked to him on the way home and he said he is really not enjoying school."

Ron was unconvinced at the time, "that boy just has to get it through his head that this behavior is unacceptable. We have to make him realize that this is serious. What kind of message are we sending him if we let him quit in kindergarten and not address his problems. He needs to know that he has to finish what he starts and he can't just run away."

Ron shook his head in dismay thinking about it now after what had transpired and having a chance to see how different things were with Nathan at his new school.

"All the things we did to him…" he looked up sadly at his wife.

"I know."

"All the times we punished him at home for bad behavior at school, all the things we took away from him."

"All the threats and all the fun I took away."

"I thought he wasn't trying but they really set him up for failure, didn't they."

"He really tried so hard. We would pull over to the side of the road a block before we got to school and he would pray to God to help him have a good day and to help him be in control. They really screwed with him."

"I can't believe I wanted him to stay to the end of the school year."

Ron recalled that first Monday evening following break after Ally had observed the classroom all day. They had sat down on the couch together after Nathan had gone to bed. Ally had been beside herself with what she had seen. She had observed for the whole day from a small room adjacent to the classroom that had windows so she could see in but the students could not see out. Because of the window placement she could not see the whole room, especially not the area just under the windows but fortunately she was able to hear most of what was happening in the room. She had taken notes all day long and had a dozen or more pages of a notebook filled with notes and comments.

"They just have no control or awareness of what is happening in the classroom," Ally started off the conversation.

"What was it like?"

"Some kids were doing fine, they just do what they are told and it is no problem but most of the time a good percentage of the class is doing something that they are not supposed to be doing and no one stops them or corrects them."

"What about all those strategies they are supposed to be using?"

"Well, I guess if you call not telling kids what kind of behaviors are not acceptable and just ignoring bad behavior a strategy then they are in full strategy mode."

"What happened?"

"I don't know where to begin. Let me just read you some of my notes. Let's see where is a good spot? Okay, here's one to start. Nathan is working in the practical life area and is singing and talking in a very loud voice, the Aide, Miss Karen, comes up behind him and says, 'Nathan use your inside voice, please'. Nathan does not react at all to her, Miss Karen repeats the request again from behind Nathan and again he has no reaction. She shrugs her shoulders and walks off. Nathan continues to talk and sing loudly."

"Oh my God, you're kidding, he didn't even react to her?"

"She never even got in front of him or down on his level so she was in his line of sight. He has no respect for her and didn't listen to a thing she said all day. And she doesn't enforce any respect or ask for any, she's worthless."

"Wow that is bad."

"It gets worse, Ron, this is not a safe environment for him." Ally paged through her notes while Ron was hit by the first of many feelings of regret over how they had handled the situation. "Here it is, you are not going to believe this, let me read it to you. Nathan is working on a math work. Toby keeps coming over and touching him and bothering him. Nathan is getting increasingly annoyed. Toby kicks Nathan in the foot. Toby spits on Nathan – in the face. Nathan starts screaming at the top of his lungs and crying. Miss Lacy comes over and talks to Nathan. I can't hear what is said but Nathan stops screaming and is calming down. Miss Lacy doesn't wipe spit off of Nathan. Toby has wandered off. Miss Lacy does not speak to or reprimand him at all."

"No way, Toby never got any kind of punishment."

"Ron, she never even wiped the spit off of Nathan's face, it was disgusting. Miss Lacy is just so unaware of what is going on. Nathan gets out of control and sometimes loses it out of frustration but Toby is a malicious child who seems to want to hurt people. Miss Lacy and Miss Karen don't do anything; it is an unsafe environment. Let me give you another example that happened later in the morning. Let me find it in my notes. Okay, here it is. Nathan is working on a work. I think it is a sound or writing exercise. He is distracted and keeps wandering away and looking at what his friends are doing but he always wanders back. He also is continually asking questions of Miss Lacy and interrupting her. She lets him interrupt. Thump. What was that? Not sure. Miss Lacy is not doing a good job of redirecting Nathan back to his work. Thump. Toby is running the length of the classroom and throwing himself against the wall underneath me. Thump. I can't see him hit the wall but I can hear it. Thump. And I can feel it. Miss Lacy seems unaware of what is going on and is not making any attempt to stop this. Thump. Toby keeps running the length of the classroom and throwing himself against the wall. Thump. Finally, Miss Lacy comes over and stops him and takes to him to the calm down table. There does not seem to be any other action taken by Miss Lacy."

"He ran the length of the room and threw himself against the wall several times and no one stopped him?"

"I don't even know if they were aware of it or they are that oblivious to most of what is going on in their classroom. This is unsafe, I don't think he can succeed in this school. You know how they told us he is worse in the afternoon and they thought it was because they separated the kindergarteners from the primary kids in the afternoon and he didn't want to do the kindergarten level works?"

"Yeah, I remember, is that not the case?"

"For starters, they leave them basically unsupervised for lunch.

Nathan hardly ate anything. He mostly wandered around to
different tables and talked to his friends or played with his food.
He ate very little out of his lunch. It is no wonder that he is
having trouble with the afternoon session, he has got to have
seriously low blood sugar."

"I don't know what to say, I'm at a loss. Anything else
happen? Was the afternoon worse or better than the morning?"

"It was better overall, but not great. They have an extra
teacher, Miss Stacy, in the room because one of the other primary
teachers joins the class in the afternoon since enough of the
primary kids only go half day that they can consolidate the
classes."

"So, she was a help in the situation."

"No, not at all, she spent the whole afternoon with one kid,
working on reading or something but really with one kid. Let me
read this to you. Nathan is in the bookshelf area and is getting
loud. Nathan just flung a book off the shelf to the ground. He is
by himself so it did not hit anyone. He flung another book. Miss
Stacy is sitting at table next to the shelves and working with same
student as before. She glances at Nathan and looks annoyed but
makes no effort to talk to him or redirect him. Nathan continues
to be loud. Now he is shouting 'help'. He is shouting 'help'
repeatedly. Nathan is on the floor, still loud, and shouting help
every 30 seconds. It has been almost 5 minutes and he is still on
the floor. Now he is shouting 'help me'. Miss Stacy is still
working with the same kid. She is about 10 feet away from
Nathan but is ignoring him and has not looked up. Now she
looks up at Nathan. She shakes her head and goes back to
working with the same student. It has been 10 minutes now. He
has also been turning in circles on the floor. The shouting is

getting less frequent. Nathan sits up, he hasn't shouted for about a minute. It has been 12 minutes since this started. Nathan is looking around and appears to realize that no one is listening to him. He gets up and wanders over to the sound area and starts on a work."

"They let him scream like that for over 10 minutes? I can't believe that. There is no way I could listen to him for that long and not do anything."

"Miss Lacy never even looked over at him or investigated to see if he did need help. Totally unsafe, we have to take him out of there. This is learned behavior, like I said before. He is learning how to behave at that school and learning how to get away with what he can get away with and they are letting him. They are totally failing him and setting him up so there is no way he can succeed. We have to get him out of there, I will call around to other schools tomorrow and see what we would have to do to get him enrolled."

They had decided that they would pull him out of Valley Ridge and enroll him in the kindergarten class at the local public school, Emerson Elementary, after Ally's day of observation and the meeting she had had with Miss Lacy and Miss Julie after school where they had both been unhelpful and dismissive towards Ally.

"I know we had to move him, but I am still surprised at how dramatic the change in him has been. I anticipated a lot more problems with the transition then with what we have seen so far."

"I know but Miss Reynolds is very good with him and very disciplined. He now knows how he should behave in the classroom and what behaviors will not be tolerated and the main key is that they enforce the rules and don't allow him to get away with anything."

"They said maybe he was not a good fit for their learning system which was one of the reasons I was so adamant for so long that he stay there and tough it out. I did a lot of research on that school and their system and they were supposed to be so good. They were right he is not a good fit for that classroom but it has nothing to do with the learning system."

"No, it is all about classroom management which they have no concept of it seems. And Miss Julie, she has no idea what she is doing, she has never been in a classroom she is not a past teacher like most administrators. I really feel sorry for the kids still in that class."

They had decided to inform the Miss Julie of their decision at the end of that first week back from vacation after the Monday observation and the arrangements for moving him to Emerson were made. Ron recalled how he had taken time off from work so that he and Ally could go in together and talk to her. That had been quite the experience.

Ally was very direct and professional about the matter, more so than could be said about any of Miss Julie's dealings with them.

"After what I saw in the classroom and after our discussion at the end of the day, we just don't think this is the right place for Nathan and are putting him in a different school. We feel that this school has failed him and us and that there are serious problems in that classroom and were disappointed that you did not want to work with us on addressing those problems."

"I'm sorry that you feel that way, and frankly I am a little shocked that you are pulling him out of school already. We made arrangements to work with you and evaluate and try any new strategies we could come up with."

"I'm sorry but we think there is a serious classroom management problem that you are not prepared to deal with."

"Well, I just want you to know that I went to bat for Nathan, when all the others didn't want to give him another chance."

Ron could see that Ally looked like she was about to get up out of the chair and strangle Miss Julie, so he decided to intervene.

"Well, we thank you for anything you may have done to help our son. But we do feel we need to pull him out of the school. I really think you should consider some of the things that Ally brought to your attention about the management of that classroom and the safety of the kids in there. I hope you don't dismiss those concerns just because you have Nathan out of there. His leaving is not going to address the other issues."

"We are constantly trying to improve our classrooms."

"Well, Ally is an expert in classroom management, if there is one thing I know for sure in this world it is that she knows what she is talking about in this area. I have seen her do some amazing things with students. If she says there are serious problems in that classroom then I would stake my life on the fact that there are serious problems in that classroom." That had about ended the discussion.

"I'm just glad we got Nathan out when we did and into a situation where he can learn and succeed. You think things will change over there... for the other kid's sake I hope so."

Ally gave him a quizzical look, "at Ridge Valley? I don't even care, but as long as Miss Julie is in charge and unless Miss Lacy starts paying attention to what is going on in her class, there is no chance. I don't even know if it is fixable, they are not doing anything right over there."

"Well they got one thing right. They were right when they said that Nathan was not a good fit for that classroom."

"No kid is a good fit for that classroom."

THE SCAPEGOAT

by: Patricia Wigeland-Clemmons

E. V. Pritchard, Private Investigator, at your service.

Oh, by the way, the E. V. stands for Ellen Valerie. It was my grandmother's name, actually, and not my idea by any means, so just call me E.V. I tell you now to resolve that question and redirect your attention on my story because this tale is not about me, or my name. This tale is about Harry Philmore.

I met Harry the day after he had been arrested on an armed robbery charge and bailed out by the local bail bondsman, a shyster named Morton Feinstein. I call Feinstein a shyster with utter conviction because I have worked for him a number of times tracking down his more errant and arrogant clients. Feinstein preferred high risk clients requiring sizeable bonds thereby collecting large on his ten per cent. Harry was no flight risk by any stretch of the imagination so I was mystified why Feinstein gave bail. You could just look at Harry and see fear, instead of sweat, emerging from every pore on his body.

Harry was a little man with a delicate bone structure most women would die for, wispy dishwater blonde hair, teary blue eyes, and limped with his left leg as he walked.

"E. V. Pritchard?" he had asked with a tentative voice after knocking lightly on my office door.

"That's me," I chirped, just to ease the tension, opening the door invitingly to Harry. "And your name is?"

"Harry. Harry Philmore," he answered, extending his hand to me.

I do loathe handshaking for the sole purpose of being social. What handshaking has become to me over my tenure as a private investigator is a lie detector. A barometer, if you will, of what is really going on inside the heart. Because of this, every handshake becomes an interrogation of the soul. The pressing of flesh, as a rule, ruins for me any future relationships. It does, however, works wonders when soul-searching seedy clients that show up with a cock 'n bull story only a fool would believe.

Harry's handshake was just as revealing as every handshake before his. His soft palms were sweaty and there was a slight tremble in the muscled part of the palm. He was scared.

"Won't you come in?"

Those watery eyes darted around my office.

"Coffee? Water?" I offered closing the door behind him. "My assistant, Hazel, is out on an errand at the moment, so it's up to me to serve you."

His eyes widened at the sound of the door latch clicking shut.

"Go ahead, have a seat."

He took one of the two used office chairs I had managed to salvage from the dumpster, courtesy of a nonpaying building tenant. Harry sat down in the chair to his right, perched on the edge of the seat like an eagle ready to take flight. Then again, maybe canary, seeing a stronger bird might be an overstatement.

"How did you come to my door, mister. . .ah, I'm sorry, your name again?"

"Philmore. Harry Philmore."

"Oh, that's right. Like the president?"

"That was Millard Fillmore with an F," he corrected me. "Mine is with a P-H."

"Right. Well, Mr. Philmore, again I ask, how did you find me?"

"Morton Feinstein."

"Morty sent you? That's unusual. He usually sends me." I replied with a hint of humor.

Oh, boy, I thought, this is going to be a good one. Wait until I get my hands on that shyster.

"Sure you don't want some coffee?" I asked as I rounded his chair and picked up the coffee pot; the brew in the bottom starting to caramelize.

"No, thank you," he answered.

I put the pot back and headed for my chair.

"What did Morty send you here for?"

"I didn't do it," he suddenly burst out. "I swear to God, I didn't do it."

I have to admit, I had heard that very line from half of my clientele, of which possibly two percent were to be believed. At this point, I had no idea what Harry Philmore had done or had not done. He could have murdered his mistress and cut her up Black Dahlia fashion or snatched the panties of the Governor's wife. I just had no idea, but by the panic in his eyes, I feared the former scenario was high on the list.

My mouth opened to ask the pivotal question when my office door opened. Hazel appeared toting two plastic grocery bags. I would have thought Harry would have jumped out of his skin at the intrusion, but after a brief flash of panic crossed his thin face, his eyes lit up at the sight of Hazel.

Now, Hazel is not the most attractive woman but she is efficient and she works to my benefit. That's not to say my matronly Hazel had completely missed the ship of wedded bliss, but it had drifted pretty far from shore.

"That highway robber at the corner convenience store raised the price on coffee again," she railed completely missing the presence of my client.

"Hazel," I interrupted. "We have company."

Hazel's head jerked up and her eyes darted to Harry. The look that passed over her face was precious and ranged from "Oh, God, what are you doing here?" to "Oh, God, what are you doing here!" Clearly, Hazel and Harry knew each other. Hazel and Harry. I mulled that name combination over in my head.

"You two know each other?"

Hazel's grocery bags fell to the floor and her mouth dropped open as Harry jumped to his feet and to her aid. They both started to talk at the same time.

"Whoa. If I were Jeremy Black, I'd bring you both in for questioning," I caution.

"Who's Jeremy Black?" Harry ask Hazel in a hushed tone.

"A detective with the Violent Crimes Unit," she whispered back, as she and Harry collected the spilled contents of the bags. "Why are you here?"

"That's what we were getting to, Hazel, when you came in." I leaned back into my chair enjoying the scramble the two were going through. "Why don't you fix us a pot of coffee, Hazel, and the three of us will have a little chat."

It was all I could do to keep a straight face. Hazel and Harry made a good couple; they both personified deer in the headlights. After the first few moments of shock, Hazel recovered nicely and became my efficient assistant again, bustling about preparing the brew. Harry took on a new personality, too, in Hazel's company and settled back into his chair, no longer the frightened canary clinging to the edge of his perch.

While the coffee dribbled through the filter, Hazel and Harry explained almost simultaneously that they met at an art fair. Somehow, this did not surprise me. Hazel being one of those women who drove me crazy with handmade cards, hand-painted flowerpots, and switch covers hand-decorated to match the color scheme of the room. Harry, well, Harry just looked like the kind who gravitated to the mild-natured souls that populated art fairs.

When Hazel blushed and Harry lowered his eyes to the floor, I knew the two were beyond the handshake stage. Teenagers would have handled the confessional better.

"Okay dokey. That explains that. Let's get to the meat of the situation here. Morton Feinstein doesn't send me clients unless his brother, Burt, wants nothing to do with the crime." I used my best stony-faced private dick glare on the both of them. "What were you bailed out for?"

"Armed robbery," Harry replied softly, cleared his throat and added, "and aggravated assault."

Hazel nervously pushed out of her chair, poured three mugs of coffee and set them on the desk.

I retrieved my hot brew. "Armed robbery? Aggravated assault? Where did this take place?"

"At a laundromat cross town."

"A laundromat ? You robbed and assaulted what? A soap dispenser?"

"I allegedly assaulted a young man by the name of Willis

Sheffield."

"Sheffield? State's Attorney Sheffield's kid?"

"Yes, ma'am."

I pushed back into my desk chair to sip my coffee. State's Attorney Anthony Sheffield was by far the most self centered, self-indulgent prick I had ever met. Odds were good his son filled out the same mold.

"I don't get it. If you assaulted this Willis kid, how the hell did you make bail?" Something didn't add up. Serious crimes, especially assault against the State's Attorney's son, went through a hearing before bond was set. Harry should still be behind bars waiting for the wheels of justice to move.

Harry shrugged.

I slipped into my detective mind set and asked, "When were you arrested?"

Harry reconstructed that night beginning with a trip to the pharmacy to pick up his mother's heart medicine, made dinner, then settled in to watch television.

"Can your mother vouch for your presence the entire night?" I knew the question was an exercise in futility. Harry had to be fifty so his mother had to be at least . . . well, old anyway.

"No, ma'am. She fell asleep about eight, I think."

"Were you told what time the crime occurred?"

"Well, during interrogation, a Detective Pierce kept pressing on me about my whereabouts at ten."

"You said Detective Pierce?"

"Yes, ma'am."

I picked up the phone and dialed the Violent Crime Unit number hoping to catch my best contact there, Jeremy Black, at his desk.

"Detective Black," the throaty voice on the other end answered.

"Hey, you busy?"

"I don't know, Evie. Depends on what you have in mind."

"I'm on the clock, but I'll give you a rain check."

He chuckled and I could hear him sandwich the handset between his shoulder and cheek, and could visualize him shuffling papers at the same time.

"I have a potential client here that I'm not clear on what the charges are."

"Doesn't he have a lawyer?"

"No. Not yet. If I knew a little more about the charges, I could hook him up with someone decent."

"Who's your client?"

"Harry Philmore with a P. H." The huge, gaping silence that

followed told me that Harry was in a world of trouble. "Black?"

"Why don't I drop by your office after work and I can collect on that rain check. We could go to Kai's for dinner and maybe take in a show."

This one-sided conversation, of course, was all crap. There was another party within earshot. Black was a football kind of guy and his idea of dinner was bratwursts and beers cooked during a tailgater at the stadium. "What time?"

Again, I could visualize him as he looked at his watch then glance at whoever was within earshot, "How about sevenish?"

"I'll be here waiting."

"Wear something red. You know how I love red," he added with a sensual murmur before hanging up.

I put the handset back on its cradle. The first time Black and I worked together was an undercover sting where I wore a wire and tried to encourage a gang lieutenant to spill some beans. "Wear something red," was a signal that the target was suspicious. "You know how I love red," was code for, it's someone I know.

It had to be Sheffield, and Sheffield had to know Harry was here. Well, there went my element of surprise.

My worst suspicions, written all over my face, made Harry suddenly resume this canary pose.

"Hazel, I need to know a little more about our victim."

I knew that Anthony Sheffield was six foot three and every bit of a fit two hundred plus pounds. It stood to reason that the boy had most, if not all, the same genes. If that were true, I needed to understand how this little guy in front of me was able to assault a kid thirty years his junior. I was not convinced Harry could manhandle Hazel without her permission, let alone a kid younger and bigger than him.

"Have you ever had a run-in with Sheffield or his family?"

Harry shook his head unconvincingly.

"Harry? Don't hold back."

"It wasn't a run-in, like you say. Years ago, he was the attorney I hired to help me in an out-of-state custody suit for my daughter."

"How many years ago?"

"Twenty some."

"Did you win?"

"No," he replied flatly. "My ex vanished with my daughter."

"You and he never had words?"

"No," he replied, his face an open book. "Barbara, my ex, just disappeared."

"How much did that set you back?"

"It was pro bono."

Even though lawyers did pro bono work to offset their shark reputations, I still could not visualize Sheffield doing it.

"I found Willis," Hazel interrupted. "He's an all-around athlete lettering in football and wrestling, graduated magna cum laude at the high school."

"Lettering? They still do that?"

"It's a private high school."

"Oh, you mean a prep school."

Goosebumps ran across the back of my neck like a herd of buffalo. Something was not right. I really needed to talk to Black, but he wouldn't be around to my door for at least, I checked my watch, another three hours.

"Okay, here's what I want you to do. Go home. Go home and take Hazel with you."

"Ah," he moaned, eyebrows knitted.

"What?" I immediately demanded.

"My mother doesn't know about Hazel."

"Time to tell her, wouldn't you say?"

"She's ill," he protested.

"So you say. She's going to get a lot sicker a lot quicker if you end up doing time. Do as I tell you and take Hazel home. I need you to be under surveillance by a friendly party that can go to court for you, if need be."

He was silent for a while, then sighed.

"I guess Mother will understand."

"What are you going to do?" Hazel asked.

"Wait for Black," I replied flatly.

After shuffling Hazel off with Harry, I sat alone in the office finishing the pot of coffee Hazel made and read the newspaper. I had little twinges of guilt for shuffling Hazel off on Harry. Harry didn't need a bodyguard, but he needed to untie the apron strings from mother. Apparently he had at one time got those strings undone long enough to have a daughter somewhere. Had the woman who bore his child caught on that old Harry was a momma's boy and split with the kid? Had she found another man with money and magic hands?

I sighed and set the last of a cold, bitter cup of coffee down and pulled a yellow, lined pad of paper out of my drawer and a half dozen pencils. I began my private brainstorm with two columns. I put Sheffield at the top of one column and Harry at the top of the other.

First, there was Willis Sheffield, the victim. Harry had beaten him in a laundromat, allegedly. Harry lived not too far from the laundromat in question; but, I wanted to know what an upscale, uptown guy like Willis was doing in a second-class neighborhood. My experience had been that the rich, and their kids, slummed for sex or drugs, both of which he could have gotten uptown. No, something else lured young Mister High-and-Tight-Pants to the laundromat.

Next in the Sheffield column was Anthony, the father.

I tapped the pencil lead on the paper and listened to my stomach growl with hunger.

State's Attorney Sheffield had run on a "tough on crime" ticket like most of the politicians in the area. All that talk seemed to do anything to reduce crime, it just made it difficult on the hard-working, honest but bumbling citizens, like Harry. That being the case, how did Harry make bail for a very serious crime before he had an attorney?

Under the Harry column, I noted that he had been with his mother that night, but Harry had no reliable corroboration for his alibi. I also made a notation about the daughter from the custody dispute from twenty years ago. If it had not been for Anthony being Harry's attorney for that dispute, I would have crossed it off the list. However, in my business, coincidences do not happen. Was there something special about that case for Sheffield to do pro bono work?

I wrote a note to Hazel in the margin of my brainstorming "look up court records on Harry's custody case."

I glanced over my sparse list again. After some thought, I circled the word bail. I wanted to know how he made bail. Looking at my watch, I found it was nearly six. I picked up the phone and dialed.

"Apex Bonding."

The voice on the other end was Rachael, Morton's daughter.

117

"Hey, young lady, don't you have a date tonight?"

She hesitated then giggled.

"No, E.V., my dad wants me to become like you. Old and unmarried."

"Well, thanks so much and may you grow hair on your chin."

She giggled again.

"Is your dad in?"

"No, he went to night court."

"Ah, damn, I forgot."

"Maybe I can help."

"Maybe. Harry Philmore was arrested for armed robbery and aggravated assault. Can you tell me why bail was set for him without a lawyer or hearing?"

"That doesn't sound right," she replied and made noises like she was thumbing through paper. "Armed robbery is pretty serious.Oh . . . kay . . . here it is," she stopped. "I wonder if I should be telling you this?"

"What? Harry's like a nobody."

She was silent again.

"The word came down from the State's Attorney's office to set bail."

"Direct from Sheffield's office?"

"Yeah, an assistant by the name of Fitzsimmons. Eileen Fitzsimmons."

Now, that was very interesting.

"Rachael, you're the best. You tell your dad, I said to let you find a boyfriend or I'm going to teach you how to shoot a gun. I know he won't like that."

Rachael giggled again.

"I don't know. I might like it, though."

We both laughed about that, then hung up.

I added the name Eileen Fitzsimmons in the column under the Sheffield heading. It might be nothing, but this kind of thing is never handled by the man himself; it's handled by a trusted assistant. I smiled. I knew Eileen and Eileen owed me a couple of favors. I really hated to use up a favor on something as trivial as Harry Philmore, but what the hell. Only live once.

There came a robust rap on the door.

"Come on in, Black. It's not locked."

The door opened and Detective Jeremy Black peered in though the partly open door, looking a little tired.

"You're early."

"Just half hour. I offered Kai's and a show," he shrugged his broad shoulders.

"I didn't wear red," I replied.

"I had a woman from upstairs standing too close for comfort."

"Eileen Fitzsimmons by chance?"

He pulled his suit coat off his muscled frame. "You must be psychic. How'd you know?"

I sighed with appreciation, thinking for a cop, a detective at that, Black had a great form. A six-foot-two frame, a handsome face, thick, black hair that begged to have my fingers run through, and deep chocolate brown eyes were exactly why I waited three hours. Delicious, I thought. Simply delicious.

"Tell you what, Black, how about we go to the sports bar around the corner and have beer and pizza. We'll talk about my client and give you an opportunity to collect the rain check."

He smiled.

"That's the best offer I've had all day."

The beer and pizza did quite a lot for us as we both relaxed. As the beer loosened our tongues, the business of comparing notes went into high gear and Detective Black laid out his information.

According to Jeremy, Detective Angel Pierce, the arresting officer, was more than vocal when his collar had been bailed out before a court appearance. When Eileen Fitzsimmons from Anthony Sheffield's office delivered the directive, it was insult to injury. Anything that involved Harry Philmore became the talk of the squad room. Additionally, Pierce reported a hysterical laundry-basket-totting Hispanic woman found the victim, beaten and unconscious. The victim, Willis Sheffield, chose silence.

Adding this information to the sketchy bit Harry had given me did nothing to resolve the puzzle.

"You know, Jeremy, I can not get over the fact that Harry knows Sheffield. Sheffield aided him in a custody dispute. Wait a minute. . .how did Pierce come to arrest Harry?"

Jeremy thoughtfully chewed his pizza before answering.

"An anonymous tip."

"How often does your unit make arrests straight away off call-in tips?"

"If the tip is righteous, we do. I can't tell you, though, because the tip came into Pierce. It must have been convincing for him to act on it."

"Who knew Harry would be home with his mother and with no alibi? How did Willis get to that laundromat? Who called the tip in and what . . . what made Sheffield go against his own 'get tough on crime' policy?"

Jeremy drained his glass of beer and motioned to the waitress to bring another.

"Am I the designated driver tonight?" I asked skeptically.

He gave me a surprised look.

"Thought that was the trade off. You drive and I spill the beans about your client."

"You son of a gun. Tell you what, you arrange to find out about Harry's ex-wife Barbara and where she disappeared to with his kid, I will not only be your designated driver, but . . ."I smiled, "I'll tuck you in bed and give you a wake up call with breakfast."

He raised an eyebrow.

"Real bacon and eggs?"

"Yep!"

He reached into his suit coat draped over the back of his chair and pulled out his cell phone. He dialed, waited, and then said.

"Need a favor. Get me information on Harry Philmore and his wife Barbara. They are divorced and she moved out of state." There was silence. "Philmore. The guy Pierce has been screaming about getting out on bail." Silence again. "That's right. That Philmore. Okay. Talk to you in the morning."

He folded the phone and tucked it in his suit coat.

"Eggs, over easy. Toast, buttered. Bacon, crisp. "He grinned at me, "A pot of coffee, black and served with a smile."

"You want it in bed, too?" I giggled.

It was six in the morning when Jeremy's phone started ringing. Blurry eyed, we both scrambled trying to find it. He found it first and I vanished into the bathroom to freshen up. Even though I had only one beer with my pizza, I made up for the difference when we settled in at my apartment. My tongue tasted like felt and my eyes did not want to stay open. I could hear Jeremy talking while I washed my face, brushed my teeth, and tried to look presentable. When I guessed nothing more could be done, I emerged as Jeremy hung up.

He was staring at the notes he had written with a curious look on his face.

"Well, spill it," I told him.

"Barbara Philmore is right here in town. She came back about six months ago."

"Really! Alone?"

"That, I don't know, but I have an address courtesy of the Department of Motor Vehicles."

"Which is?"

"About two blocks from the laundromat."

"How many eggs do you want?"

"Two plus four strips of bacon."

Jeremy was proud of himself for finding the information for me, but I was realistic. So many times, the DMV addresses were nonexistent. After we ate, he offered to accompany me to see this Barbara Philmore.

At first, I resisted but then decided that maybe it would not hurt to have a witness to this curious phenomenon. Before we left, though, I called Hazel and instructed her to collect Harry and bring him to the address. I made no effort to tell her why, just to meet me there. I needed to know if my client was lying about not knowing where his ex-wife was and I needed to know for Hazel's sake. Next, I called Eileen Fitzsimmons and left a message that I had a lead on Harry's ex-wife and where to meet me. I figured either Anthony or Eileen would show up.

"You know," Jeremy cautioned me as I locked my apartment door and headed to the stairwell with him by my side, "that only works in the movies."

"Well. . .now. . .see, you burst my bubble!"

It might only work in the movies, I reasoned, but this was beginning to look like something a scriptwriter could not possibly make up.

On the ground floor, we climbed into my Honda Accord and drove across town to the address provided by the DMV. It turned out to be a little white house that had a postage stamp front yard, no fence, no flowers and a beat up blue, mid-nineties Buick Roadmaster in the driveway. If the car had not been there, I would have assumed no one was home. I parked my Accord and proceeded to the front door. I reached to push the doorbell button when the door flew open.

"Don't touch that!"

The voice was that of a tall, red-haired woman. Her hair, pulled back and coiled into a bun, had loose graying strands flying free.

"What do you want?" she demanded.

"I'm looking for Barbara Philmore," I stated, barely getting the words out.

"Who wants her?"

I reached into my pants pocket and produced a business card, handing it to her.

"So," she sneered and flipped the card back at me. "I got no business with a private. . .dickless," she snarled.

"Momma! You be nice!"

The voice behind Momma was a sweet-sounding young woman. She stepped around Momma.

"I'm sorry, Momma is suspicious of strangers."

"We are here looking for Barbara Philmore."

"Well," the small, blonde woman began ,stepping between Momma and me. "We are both named Barbara."

The little woman standing in front of me was a dead ringer for Harry. She had the same delicate bone structure in the face, same wispy blonde hair, and same teary blue eyes. On her, it looked pretty good.

I heard two cars pull up behind us, but I kept my eyes on both women.

"Barbara?" I heard Harry call. "Barbara, is that you?"

The younger Barbara looked puzzled while the older one took on the features of rage. As Harry climbed the steps, the older Barbara thrust herself through the door at Harry. Lucky for Harry, Jeremy and I were in her way. As if on cue, Eileen pulled up. Guess she didn't want her boss getting bad publicity out of this.

Jeremy and I had the older Barbara tackled and face down. Eileen marched up to the stoop, "Barbara! Stop it!"

As if somebody flipped the switch, the older woman stopped her struggling. Jeremy and I hoisted Barbara to her feet. She took one look at Harry and burst into tears.

I looked at Jeremy, he looked at me, and we both said, "I'm afraid to ask."

"I'm sorry, E.V. I tried to get things straightened out, but Barbara is a little off. " Eileen began apologetically. "She attacked Mr. Sheffield's son and then turned Harry in for the crime."

"Why did she attack Willis?"

Eileen sighed and took me by the elbow. "I'm telling you this, but if I hear it anywhere else, I will deny it." Eileen cleared her throat. "Barbara believes her daughter is Mr. Sheffield's daughter. It was her way of retribution. "

I turned to look at the younger Barbara who was trying to placate her mother and shyly talking to her father at the same time.

"I know there is no resemblance. Years ago, Mr. Sheffield was having an affair with Barbara when she became pregnant. She has been threatening to expose him still claiming Mr. Sheffield is Barbara's father."

"Why assault Willis?"

"Jealousy, I guess. She called the boy and gave some vague story about an ongoing affair his father was having. Willis thought he would be safe by meeting her in a public place, but Barbara laid in wait for him with an aluminum bat. By involving Willis, she was trying to bring attention to Mr. Sheffield and she hated Harry enough to set him up for the assault. The woman is demented."

"So poor old Harry ended up the scapegoat twenty years ago and again a few days ago. And what did Sheffield plan to do to solve this one?"

"I set up to get him bailed and instructed Morton Feinstein to send him to you." She shrugged. "I knew you would figure this mess out. Get Harry off the hook; even bring father and daughter together without Mr. Sheffield's involvement."

"So, what about Barbara's Momma?"

"I can keep her out of the picture if you and Harry can keep her under wraps."

"Me and Harry? For God's sake, am I a miracle worker?"

Eileen glanced in Harry's direction. Hazel was standing next to Harry acting very businesslike, but I could see she was holding

Harry's hand while he talked to the younger Barbara.

"Fine. You tell that boss of yours, he owes me a favor," I said, wishing Hazel had not fallen head over heels for Harry. "To be redeemed at a later date for something of equal value."

Eileen gave me a worried look.

I clapped her on the back and winked.

"Nothing material , Eileen. I restore the lost, the stolen, and the misused, be it lives, loves, or reputations. But you tell Sheffield for me, no more scapegoats."

Eileen nodded. "I guarantee it."

CHANGING PERCEPTIONS

by: Katherine Lato

Snowball didn't want to sit on Carli's lap despite the lovely full back massage. He purred, but squirmed to get off. Carli finally let go, and Snowball headed for a good hiding place.

The room with the funny blinking machine was usually quiet this time of day. Since the room was spotless, Snowball knew he wouldn't be chased by the noisy robotic vacuum cleaner, nor inadvertently sprayed with cleaning fluid. He'd sniffed cleaning fluid, so knew that the peaceful afternoon was about to be shattered.

* * *

"Carli! Your room is a mess!"

Hiding inside the Topper Bonnet in Mom's office to avoid Mom's cleaning rampage, Carli admired the silk holographic cover she'd installed on the inside. Carli doubted Mom had ever noticed it.

Mom wouldn't think to look for her inside, not after all her lectures about not touching anything in her office. She acted like Carli was a little kid who didn't know how to behave around the thought and reason machine, instead of a wise thirteen. If Mom paid proper attention to the latest styles, she would know that Carli used expensive imaging devices in her fashion class. She could be trusted with a machine, even a complicated one like the Topper Bonnet.

Since Carli couldn't come out until Mom's four o'clock appointment, she wished she'd brought the cat in. Not that he would have stayed. Snowball adored Dad, and jumped into his lap constantly although Dad usually shoved him away because he was busy performing calculations on his computer. When Carli scooped Snowball up, he rarely settled, no matter how much she stroked him.

Carli was bored, so she looked in the small notebook where Mom usually wrote down her password. Just for fun, she typed in the login and password. She put on the 3-D trifocals with her mind full of an image of Snowball cuddling on her lap, purring. She had a sudden vision about what to change to get him to treat her differently.

Carli and her sister had named the large machine that occupied half of Mom's home office the Topper Bonnet back when Mom had a smaller version that just went over her head. The current model didn't look like a bonnet, being metal and full of blinking lights, but Mom smiled the first time they called it a Topper Bonnet, and the name stuck. Not that Mom smiled while using the Topper Bonnet since she believed that emotion ruined her scientific experiments.

Mom walked around the house without expression for half an

hour before she stepped inside the machine. Carli stayed away from her then. Mom would talk, but she sounded like a robot, saying no to everything, even logical requests like an increase in clothing allowance. Mom's work was tedious despite her lofty claims about the joy of pursuing pure science and keeping emotions out of the equation.

Discussions with Mom about emotion versus science annoyed Carli, although not as much as arguing about schoolwork, friends, money, free time and practically everything else. Mom claimed it was because Carli was a teenager, but it had more to do with Mom not paying attention to things like clothing, or shoes. Mom said that pure science didn't care what she looked like. Carli thought Mom should take a little pride in her appearance.

Carli took off the glasses. She called up the log file, carefully deleting her presense in the machine. It made her feel a little guilty, but she hadn't really done anything wrong. Mom's experiments didn't have anything to do with Snowball.

During the following week, the change in the cat was wonderful. After just the one time imagining the cat snuggling, Snowball now wanted to be in Carli's lap more than Dad's. The rest of the family didn't even notice. Her sister was busy trying to decide what area of Business Studies to pursue, so dinner conversation centered on her options, with Mom and Dad having their usual boring discussions about pure science.

As the largest of their three moons was coming into near cycle, Mom said, "Carli, if you don't clean your room, you'll stay behind when the rest of us go moon exploring."

Since moon exploration only came up every few months, Mom used the approaching outing to get the girls to do their chores.

Carli disliked her mother's manipulation, and her room wasn't that messy. Even Dad claimed that Mom's standards were unreasonable at times.

Carli dumped the cat from her lap, resigned to cleaning up her room. Before she stood, she heard Mom's corporate funding device chime. She waited to see if Mom would be distracted.

* * *

Snowball rubbed his nose against Carli's legs. He wanted her to sit back down so he could cuddle. He loved cuddling with Carli. Even more than with the tall one or any of the other occupants of the house.

"Oh, dear, what's wrong now?" Mom asked.

Snowball felt the wonderful sensation of being scooped up by Carli. This was more like it.

* * *

Carli grinned. Since Mom had expressed emotion, she wouldn't be using her machine. In fact, she'd gone to the kitchen muttering that she might as well try that new recipe for yogurt cake. Dad was at the office and her sister was emailing gushy letters to her boyfriend on Alpha Centauri. They weren't very gripping; 'I miss you' and 'Remember that time when we saw the two sunrises from the planet with binary suns?' But Josie was utterly captivated by them, so wouldn't notice that Carli was in Mom's office.

Dad joked that Mom possessed a clean gene that made her spot dirt the rest of them couldn't see. Life would be more pleasant if that trait was removed. Once again, Carli wasn't sure exactly how the Topper Bonnet worked, but she felt warmth and a satisfied glow and knew she'd been successful in changing Mom's behavior.

At dinner that evening, her parents had a heated argument about the ethics and the morality of something or other. Instead of changing the subject to the newest version of multiple sensation fabric, Carli paid attention. If she understood more about Mom's work, she'd be able to help her. From what she could tell, Mom was trying to invert a homogeneous cylinder by genetic algorithm and mutation.

Mom's voice became sharp when Carli asked questions. "Be polite. I know the newest fashion magazine came out on the vid today, but you can wait to discuss it until Dad and I finish. I'm at a tricky bit and need his advice."

"I didn't ask about fashion," Carli said. "I asked why you were inverting the cylinder."

"You've never shown much enthusiasm about science before." Mom narrowed her eyes, studying Carli who innocently munched on a roll. "Since when are you curious about my work?"

Carli swallowed her bread. "You're having trouble using the Topper Bonnet to influence the shape mutation. What, exactly, are you trying to do? Maybe there's an easier way to get the result you want if you'd explain without all the gobbly-gook language." Carli cut her chicken flavored protein stick into tiny pieces to avoid Mom's piercing gaze.

Mom pursed her lips, clearly suspecting that Carli was just trying to be difficult. "Numerical simulation shows that, even with a bad initial guess, good reconstruction can be obtained as long as the noise level is within range. I'm working to decrease the noise level via the Demagnifying Simulation Control--the Topper Bonnet as you girls named it."

"Mom does important work," Josie said. "Let her and Dad talk about it."

Carli glared at her sister. "I'm interested."

"That's very sweet of you, Carli. Now eat your dinner."

"And you'd better clean up your room," Dad said. "We want to visit the moon tomorrow."

Mom waved her hand. "Her room is fine. There's no need to be over the top on cleanliness."

Struggling to hide her smile at the shock on the faces of Dad and Josie, Carli pretended she wanted a second helping of green beans. She'd done it again, and now she wanted to use her new-found ability to fix Mom's problem.

Carli waited until she was alone in the apartment a few days later before approaching the machine. There might be a reason why Mom was careful to remove all emotion before using the machine, but Carli wasn't her mother. She approached life differently.

Carli concentrated on the noise level, visualizing it as a lower number than the one she'd scribbled down and memorized. There was no sense of accomplishing what she wanted, maybe because it was a number. Carli tried to visualize it as a graph, but that didn't help. With the cat, she'd pictured him on her lap, and how good it felt, and suddenly, she'd done it. With Mom, she'd imagined her room as a total mess, and Mom giving her a hug anyway. Both times, she'd pictured herself happy once the change was made.

It was hard to picture being happy with a lower noise level for the third quadrant in the right frame. Because she was bored and wanted to borrow her sister's fuzzy sweater, she imagined Josie sharing her things. Almost immediately, she got the familiar wash of joy and warmth. She turned back to the number. If the noise level in the third quadrant went lower, life would be wonderful. Once again, the wave of joy and warmth engulfed her. She'd done it. At least, she thought she had.

When Carli heard a knock on her door a few hours later, she hoped it was Mom wanting to talk. Carli could find out if her experiment was successful without making Mom suspicious.

It was Josie, holding a pink sweater. "You wanted to borrow this, right?"

"I thought you were afraid I'd drop food on it."

"Sorry about that," Josie said. "I don't know why I treat you like a little kid."

"Because I'm younger than you?"

"Well, yeah, but you're not a little kid." Josie held out the fuzzy garment. "Don't you want the sweater? You've been bugging me about it for weeks."

"Thanks." Carli held the sweater up and studied herself in the mirror, trying to remember why she'd thought it would look good on her.

"Girls! Time for dinner!"

After walking into the dining room, Carli stared at the table set with a white tablecloth. A vase of pink and lavender sunflowers decorated the center and white candles flickered in the evening light.

"Mom!" Josie exclaimed. "You ordered Cexaria's Special! What are we celebrating?"

"Sit down, girls," Dad said. "Once you hear what she's achieved, I hope you're as proud of your brilliant mother as I am."

Carli's stomach felt funny, and not in a good way. She should admit what she'd done, while Mom could fix her tampering.

Mom's face glowed as she passed around the seventeen dishes that were part of Cexaria's Special. Normally Carli and Josie fought over the extra cinnamon-flavored protein stick, but tonight Josie offered it to Carli.

"I don't want it," Carli said. "I ate two last time."

"That's all right. I know they're your favorite."

"They're your favorite, too."

"If neither of you want it, I'll take it," Dad said.

Josie smiled. "They are good, aren't they?"

"The best."

The cinnamon flavor tasted like ashes to Carli, but she managed to chew and swallow. Her stomach continued to churn with anxiety, and she avoided looking at Mom.

After they'd all eaten a little, Dad raised his water glass. "I'd like to propose a toast." He waited until they all raised their glasses. "To Eileen, and her breakthrough in science. You did it, dear! You persisted despite the skeptics, and you've demonstrated that your method works."

"It will have to be duplicated independently."

"It will be." He kissed her cheek. "You've kept marvelous notes. How long do you think it will take?"

"I contacted James this afternoon. It will probably take a week, maybe two."

"In time for the next quarterly publication. You'll be famous."

"Well, not really famous."

"This is a major breakthrough, and you accomplished it on your own." His eyes twinkled and the dimples in his cheeks deepened with delight. "Girls, aren't you going to tell your mother how proud of her you are?"

"This is great!" Josie clapped her hands together. "You've been working on this problem for five years, right?"

"Six. I tried every combination. So many times I almost gave up, but I just knew that this would work out."

"You're amazing." Josie kicked Carli's leg under the table.

When Carli looked up, Josie mouthed the words, 'say something.'

"Yes, you're amazing, Mom." Carli considered confessing what she had done, but she might as well let Mom enjoy her evening. She could tell her tomorrow. "May I be excused?"

"You haven't finished your cinnamon protein stick, or the flat bread. Are you feeling all right?"

"My stomach hurts."

Mom put her hand on Carli's forehead. "You don't have a temperature. Go lie down, and I'll be in shortly to check on you."

Walking into her bedroom, Carli wanted to be alone. If she confessed what she'd done, the light in Mom's eyes would disappear. Mom hadn't been this happy in a long time. She would tell her tomorrow. She could picture how angry Mom would be, and how disappointed to learn that her breakthrough was because of emotion. It was a mess, and it was all her fault.

Maybe she could fix it herself. If she used the Topper Bonnet one last time, she could reverse--reverse what? Carli didn't understand the scientific principles behind Mom's work, since she'd always dismissed it as boring. Still, with time inside the Topper Bonnet, she could fix this.

The next morning, Carli walked into Mom's study, hoping to find the Topper Bonnet free. Mom wasn't around, but neither was her machine.

Carli wanted to ask Dad about the machine, but was worried she'd make him suspicious, so she asked, "Where's Mom?"

"At her office. She had an early morning interview with a major publication. They're releasing an abstract of her paper today, and want her to promote it."

"Today? So fast? Wait, Mom doesn't have an office."

"She does now. Your mother made a scientific breakthrough. One that has been a long time coming. This is going to cause things to change around here." He stared out the window, apparently lost in thought. "Big changes. For one thing, your mother will be busier than ever. She won't be able to set her own schedule. It means we'll have to all pitch in and help around the house."

"Did she take the Topper Bonnet to her office?"

"Yes. We moved it first thing this morning. Why?"

"No reason."

Her voice must have reflected her dismay, since Dad looked at her carefully. "Is something wrong?"

Carli couldn't face his concerned gaze. He wasn't the one she needed to tell. Her parents were big on not going to the easier parent; she and Josie had to talk to the one most involved in the decision, not try to get the other parent on their side. "Nothing. I have to review a report for school."

"You could be a bit more enthusiastic about your mother's success. Even if you don't understand the details of how the Demagnifying Simulation Control works, you're old enough to appreciate that her hard work has finally paid off. Maybe this will help you see that the intellectual pursuit of pure science has a place in our world, despite what the emotionalists think. I know it's not fashion, but you could act interested."

"I am," Carli said. "Fashion isn't my only concern. What do you mean about the emotionalists? What do they have to do with Mom's work?"

His explanation used words that Carli thought she understood. However, they were in combinations that made no sense. What did a cultural universe have to do with anything? She also didn't understand what 'measuring the semantic structure of emotion' meant or how emotion and related unconscious cognitive processes played a role in Mom's experiments.

Once Dad's attention turned to his computer, she wandered into her bedroom and laid down on the bed.

After five minutes, she heard a scratching at the door. When she opened it, the cat walked into her room, purring loudly. She left the door slightly open.

"Come here, you," Carli picked up Snowball, setting him next to her on the bed. "Do you really like me, or is it because I changed your behavior?"

The cat purred.

Carli curled around the cat, wishing that she didn't feel like crying. Or that she could cry and get rid of the bad feelings. She held the cat closer which used to make him squirm until she let him go. Today he purred loudly.

Her door opened wider and Josie walked in. "Let the cat go. Snowball doesn't like being snuggled so closely."

* * *

Snowball was aware of the sisters talking, but as long as Carli continued to hold him, he was content.

"He doesn't mind," Carli said. "What are you doing in my room?"

"Your door was open. Let Snowball go."

From Josie's tone of voice, Snowball knew that she was ordering her sister to do something. Why couldn't she leave them alone? Snowball had found the perfect warm spot on Carli's lap, and now he was being shifted. He blinked twice, then laid his head on her pillow.

"That's weird. I wonder if he'll sit on my lap?" Josie stood in front of the mirror, twisting her hair back from her face.

"Aren't you going to try?" Carli asked.

"I can wait until he moves. He looks comfortable next to you."

Snowball felt Carli pick him up. He started to purr loudly, hoping that she would snuggle against him again, but Carli handed him to her sister.

Josie sat on the edge of the bed. Her stroking was all wrong, making his fur ruffle. Snowball squirmed until Josie removed her hands. He jumped off the bed, walking to the door.

* * *

Josie shook her head. "Sorry I disturbed him."

"It's fine. Did you want something?"

"Dad said you were asking questions about Mom's work. Are you worried how her success is going to change things?"

"Are you?" Carli asked.

"A little. Mom worked hard on her hypothesis, and it's great that she made a breakthrough, but what if she can't duplicate it?" Josie picked up a book from Carli's desk. "Then again, I'm sure Mom ran the test multiple times before getting excited about the results since she's very methodical about her work. That's why I want a career in business. With all that time and energy, Mom should be making breakthroughs regularly."

Deciding that not asking questions was likely to make Josie suspicious, Carli asked, "What if there was something unique about yesterday that made Mom's experiment work, and she can't duplicate it?"

"Then she'll spend another six years working on it." Josie set the book down. "All for a few weeks of success. It makes me wonder if Mom is wrong about there being such a split between the intellectual and the emotional."

"What do you mean?"

"In business, things are never one hundred percent one way or another. I wonder if it's similar in Mom's work, and that's why it's been such a struggle." Josie shrugged. "Not that Mom will ever see the error of her ways."

"Mom does change her mind," Carli said. "Like she finally let you date Alexier."

"True. After months of my asking. If she didn't work on her own, another person might be able to influence her, look at the latest research and draw parallels. It would be sad if all her work was for nothing."

Carli struggled to keep her expression blank, but some of her disquiet must have shown.

"You don't look so good," Josie said. "Are you feeling all right?"

"My stomach hurts."

"Should I get Dad?"

"No," Carli said. "I'm going to rest."

"All right. Do you want a cup of tea? I have a little of the white pear Grandma sent me. I could make you a cup."

It was Josie's favorite drink, one that she rarely shared. Carli tried to smile, but only managed a weak, "No thanks."

"It will be all right."

Life would never be all right again. Carli wished there was something she could do other than confessing that she'd fiddled with the Topper Bonnet. It seemed too late to tell Mom everything.

When Mom returned from her interview, Carli cleaned her

room daily, but Mom didn't even notice. She was busy going into the office daily.

As the weeks passed, Mom's enthusiasm was replaced by grim determination. Most conversation at dinner was about work. Carli avoided interrupting. Even Josie rarely brought up the latest business news.

"I don't understand it," Mom said. "I've run the sequence a hundred times, but it isn't working. I need an assistant to see if the first set was a fluke. The variations are so small, once I set the main parameters, a monkey could run these tests."

"I think all the monkeys are busy rewriting Shakespeare," Dad said.

Usually his corny jokes made Mom laugh, or her eyes twinkle. Today she merely nodded, evidently taking him seriously.

Dad patted Mom's hand. "You'll figure it out. You're good at that."

"Maybe I should have gone into something easy like biospace engineering."

"Take a break. The problem will still be there tomorrow."

"That's what I'm afraid of," Mom said. "I don't know what I'm doing wrong, and I'm running out of ideas. Sometimes, I sit inside the machine, trying to reconstruct what I did when it worked, but my mind just drifts. It was easier when I was home since I didn't worry about the girls."

"You can trust us," Josie said.

Her parents looked up, as if surprised Josie and Carli were eating dinner with them.

"I'm sorry," Mom said. "This must be boring."

To Carli's surprise, Josie shook her head. "I know this matters. I wish I'd taken self-motivation in my business seminar, so I could help you. I'm starting to wonder if we'll ever get to the really good stuff. Business may not be as fascinating as I used to think. Anyway, you don't need to worry about Carli and me."

"Thank you. It's not really you. I keep looking for a reason to explain my lack of progress. I can't clear my head of distractions by taking a walk like I used to at home, since someone always stops to ask a question about funding or another issue that wrecks my concentration." Mom shook her head. "I don't know what to do."

"You could bring the machine back home," Carli said. "Then I could help."

"I'm afraid not. It's sweet of you to offer, but it would require special training. You've only taken the minimal math classes despite our encouragement."

"I took math," Josie said, "for my business classes, so I could help."

"Aren't you studying for your placement exam?" Dad picked up a bowl. "Does anyone mind if I finish the mashed potatoes?" At the shake of heads, he scooped the potatoes onto his plate.

"I'll do fine," Josie said. "Even if I don't get into business school this year, I can study basic math which is a good basis for many careers."

Carli needed access to the machine to undo her changes. "I'd like to help. I thought you said a trained monkey could run the tests."

"I may have exaggerated," Mom said. "It does take scientific knowledge to run the equipment. Really, girls, we don't have to talk about my work all the time. Did anything interesting happen today?"

"My school is offering an internship in a variety of science fields," Carli said. "If I took one of them, would I be able to help?"

"I thought you planned to study fashion," Mom said. "While Josie's field overlaps in the math area, there's not much crossover with fashion and science. Only in fabric composition, and I didn't think you wanted to pursue that."

"I can do both," Carli said.

Mom raised her eyebrows in surprise, then touched Carli's arm gently. "Make sure it's a field you're interested in. Your father and I want you girls to choose careers that you're excited about."

Her consideration only increased the guilt churning inside Carli. Even if Carli told Mom about using the Topper Bonnet with emotion, She might not believe her. Carli had casually mentioned the Emotional Quantum Relevance Theory, but Mom dismissed it as pseudo-science.

Carli wanted to do something. "I can at least check it out."

"Me too," Josie said.

"That would be great. I'm proud of you both, no matter what you do, but your wanting to help makes me happy." Mom's eyes were bright, as if she was about to cry. She stood up. Her hug felt extra good.

Although the classes were boring at first, Carli forced herself to answer as many questions as she could. With serious studying in the evenings, and on the weekends, she was among the top students in her session. When Dr. Prowstern picked her for an internship, her parents were clearly proud of her. Their praise lessened her feelings of guilt, but she wanted to do more. She owed it to her mother for fiddling with her machine. The more she learned about how the machine worked, at least how Mom hoped it would work with pure reason, the more aghast Carli became at her earlier behavior.

A few months later, she was about to walk into the living room where her parents were sitting on the sofa. Carli realized they were talking about her and Josie, so she paused to eavesdrop.

"I know what you mean," Dad said. "Although I always thought that if we gave them time to get over their adolescent fancies, they might be drawn into the scientific field."

"It's more than I dared hope," Mom said.

"Hope? Careful, dear, you're becoming emotional about this issue."

"Oh, you." Mom tossed a cushion at him. "I'm not such a cold fish."

"I never said you were a cold fish. Come closer and I'll prove it."

Carli backed out of the room, not wanting to see where their light-hearted discussion would take them next. Parents could be so immature.

***

It took time and effort, but Mom's pleasure at Carli's interest made her study of the intellectual approach worthwhile. Mom explained her work carefully, repeating key parts. Unfortunately, she refused to bring the machine home so Carli was never alone with the Demagnifying Simulation Control machine.

Hoping there was a way to shift Mom's thinking without the machine, Carli studied hard in school. For a while, she kept up with fashion design as well, but there were conflicts. One semester she could only study pure science or fashion, not both. Carli switched her planned field of study from Clothing to Science.

She stopped paying attention to her own attire. It was easier to just grab a clean shirt and a pair of slacks and it didn't matter anyway. She was close to making a breakthrough. Why she'd ever thought that it was easier to use emotion in science was beyond her. Mom was right. The intellectual side was way more challenging.

Carli couldn't wait to talk about her latest discovery at dinner. It would be a fascinating discussion, especially since Josie was in the middle of an advanced graphing class and might offer valuable insight.

* * *

Snowball meowed. Why didn't Carli have time for him anymore? Instead of sitting in her lap, Snowball often had to duck to avoid being kicked. Carli was muttering something about, "Having important things to do. She had science to pursue."

Snowball purred. He didn't care about science. He wanted to snuggle with Carli.

Infinite Monkeys

JUST APPETIZERS

by: Barry Glicklich

Walter Isaacs parked his Audi TT in the usual spot outside the restaurant and hurried inside, his woolen suit jacket providing incomplete protection against the chill of a Chicago winter.

He smiled at the hostess as he walked by her and turned left into the open expanse of the bar area. Studying the daily special board nestled below the vast stainless steel tanks containing the coming month's special brews, he didn't notice Melissa's approach until she was close enough to reach out and give him a hug.

"How cold does it have to get before you put on a coat? What would your mother say?" Melissa released him and plucked a small bit of lint from Walter's shoulder as she stepped back.

Walter ran his fingertips along the side of his smooth-shaven face until they joined with his thumb directly below the chin and laughed. "The same thing she always says. You're a grown-up now, so I'm not going to tell you what to do."

He stepped up into a small booth. "I have one in the car, just in case. Besides, it's over two hundred and fifty degrees out there, if you measure in Kelvin. Once it drops below that, I usually carry the coat."

Melissa leaned over the table, her dark brown hair creeping over her shoulder and swinging down to within an inch of the table surface. "Do you know what you'll be having today? I checked, and we still have a little bit of the stout on cask."

"Was that the Irish stout or a milk stout?"

"The milk. Tim had trouble with the nitrogen tank on the Irish stout and had to toss an entire batch."

Walter wrinkled his nose in response. "Ouch. That must have given the manager heartburn."

"Only a little bit. Francine is the current corporate lackey who acts like she's in charge at this point. But she'll probably find a way to blame the problems on the previous guy and take credit for the things that go well so she can move on to some more prestigious branch."

"Could be. It's hard for me to remember that this is part of a chain. To me, it's always Melissa's place."

"But I'm just a waitress here and it's the corporation that provides those promotions you like so much. I presume that you have another coupon for a free appetizer?"

"I do. And I think I'll have the potato soup with toast points today."

"Sounds good. I'll get that order in. Do you have to go to court this afternoon, or can you allow yourself a little beer?"

"My dad has me reviewing the files from a couple of key clients so I'll be up to speed if he wants to pull me in. Since it's just reading, and no direct client interaction, I should be good for at least a pint today."

"In that case, I'll bring you samples of the stout, the ale, and the wheat, to help you decide." She gave a stage wink before straightening up and heading toward the kitchen.

Walter watched Melissa sway as she walked away. He knew that much of the effect was a deliberate ploy to increase the tips she received from her male customers. He respected that it worked well, and though he felt that he had moved beyond that in his friendship with her, it didn't mean he couldn't enjoy the view.

Two days later, Walter pushed through the glass door leading into the restaurant and stopped at the hostess stand, scanning the polished wood surface in search of a listing of table assignments, until the hostess straightened up from the glass-covered diagram of the restaurant tables and set down the wax pencil.

"Good afternoon, can I help you? Would you like a table for one?"

"That depends. Is Melissa not in today?"

The hostess leaned over her tablet. "Yes, she is here. She's working cocktail. It's just ---"

"Thanks. I know the way." Walter gave a tip of an imaginary hat as he turned out of the entry hall. Beyond the clusters of people perched on stools surround the high round tables in the center of the lounge, he spotted Melissa by the coffee brewing machines.

"Oh good, you are here. I didn't see your car out front."

Melissa rubbed her index fingers from the corner of her eyes across her cheeks, following a faint path of mascara that had previously mapped the route. "Yes, well, I am here." She turned away from him and walked over to his usual booth and sat down with an audible thud on the dark wooden bench. "Pardon me if I sit, but I'm drained. What can I get you?"

A set of wrinkles lined up in the space between his eyebrows and his hairline as he reached for her hand. "You can tell me what's got you so down. I'd offer to buy you a drink, but I know how management frowns on staff taking advantage of the craft brews while on duty."

Melissa stared down at the surface of the table and tightened her hand into a fist inside Walters hand. "I'll try to get through this without bawling this time. This will be the fifth time today, so I should be getting good at it." She looked up at Walter.

With a direct view, he could see that her eyes were red and veined, and there were dark shadows beneath the lower lids.

She took a deep breath and retracted her hand, laying it with the other hand palm down on the table in front of her. "I was out last night with a friend for dinner and a movie. He drove. When we got back to my apartment, the door was open a crack, and my place had been robbed. My laptop, my iPod, a fur coat I had been given by my grandmother that I never wore- they were all gone." She lifted her hand from the table, pinched her nostrils together, and ran the back of her right hand out away from her eye. "They even took a suitcase that I had been given as a going away present when I went to France for a year abroad. It had everybody's signatures on it."

Pulling a crumpled and sodden tissue from her pocket, she blew her nose. "We called the police, and they came out, and while they were asking questions, I checked my spare set of car keys and found that my car had been stolen!"

Walter reached into the left lower pocket of his suit coat and pulled out a stack of tissues. Unfolding it, he divided the pile in two and slid one half toward Melissa. "How awful! Did you consider skipping work today?"

She pulled the tissues toward herself, removing the top layer and rubbing her nose with it. "I can't afford to! Before this, I could barely afford my rent, and tuition, and as it stands, I can't take on another monthly payment, so I'll probably have to give up my apartment, since I still have six months left on the lease. Or I could put my degree on hold ... AGAIN!"

"Is there anything I can do to help?"

"That's sweet, Walter, but I really couldn't take anything from you. And in fact, I'd better get you a menu and a drink, or I won't have a job. We have a buffalo chicken wrap appetizer that is supposed to be really good. Can I get you started with a couple of sample beers?"

Later that afternoon back in his office, Walter hung up the phone and scribbled a note in his calendar to call the Assistant States Attorney back again in a couple of days.

Pleased that he'd found a way to help Melissa, Walter scanned through the computer file he had started with the details of her robbery. After the report had been filed, the police had updated the state-wide database of stolen vehicle and the county pawn shop records. Two days later, the transponder for automatic charging of tolls had set off an alert, and when the car had exited the toll system at Maple avenue, it had taken only a couple minutes for the car to be located and pulled over.

The alleged perpetrator was 19-year old kid, and this was his first felony charge.

Walter pictured Melissa's reaction, and suspected that she wouldn't feel particularly vindicated if he were imprisoned. More to the point, it wouldn't alleviate her financial difficulties. He gazed out the window of his office, watching the bare branches quivering high overhead. With a start, he recalled an attorney who had given a guest lecture at his law school a couple years ago on the process of establishing a restorative justice program in the county.

After struggling to recall the lawyer's name, he turned back to his computer to request a search for DuPage, Illinois, and "restorative justice program". Within a minute, he was on the phone, holding for Sylvia Gulbranson.

The following Thursday, Walter ducked his head into the wind as he crossed the parking lot to the entrance, arriving at the restaurant a few minutes before noon.

Stepping in to the spacious foyer, he shook off the cold as he took a breath, inhaling the mixed scents of fermenting beer and grilling onions. A moment later, he was greeted by Melissa's chiding smile "Warm enough for you out there?." The smile faded and her eyebrows narrowed as she glanced back at the hostess, took a step toward him and dropped her voice to barely above a whisper. "I'm not sure what's up. The manager didn't assign me a section, and when I asked about it, he said that I should hang around and help out where I can." She blinked twice in rapid succession as her voice quavered, "I hope they're not about to lay me off, because that would be the last straw."

Walter lifted a hand and gave her left shoulder a gentle squeeze. "It's fine, and I didn't mean to add to your stress."

Melissa pulled her head back and widened her eyes as Walter continued. "I have a business meeting today, and I didn't want you bringing me over a pint of espresso stout as soon as I walked in the door, as you have been known to do at times. And under most circumstances, I am very grateful for it.

"Second, the meeting includes you. I asked your manager if I could cover your wages for an hour during today's lunch, and he was very supportive once I explained the situation. You have nothing to be worried about with respect to your work here. They hold you in high regard."

Walter extended his ring finger to join the first two that were pointing to the floor of the bar. "Third, I wanted a few minutes to tell you what this meeting is about."

"Shall we get a table and establish our home-turf advantage?"

Turning back to the hostess, Walter indicated that he wanted a booth for four, ignoring Melissa's curious gaze.

Stepping back to allow Melissa in first, he slid next to her and turned his head to face her. "The police told you that they found the person who broke into your apartment."

She nodded. "Yes, and thankfully I have my car again, though it's much worse for the wear. I can't even open the passenger door from the dent in the side. Unfortunately, I didn't have comprehensive coverage on my insurance, and I have some other stuff that has to be replaced first. The cops said that they're still working on locating the laptop and suitcase and other stuff, but they don't have a lot of hope."

Walter nodded. "That's what I've been told also. But I've taken things a step further. Have you ever heard the term 'restorative justice'?"

Melissa shook her head.

"It starts from the idea that for a crime that involves two parties, both the offender and the victim should play a part in resolving it. A key part of this is direct interaction between the two parties. It can give the victim a chance to confront the offender and understand their circumstances, and it shows the offender the direct effects of his actions and how those actions caused his victim pain and suffering. From a legal perspective the roots go back over four thousand years. But it was largely replaced by retributive justice - punishing the offender for the last thousand years.

"In addition to being an effective way of preventing future crime by the offender, which is good for society, it gives the victim an opportunity to receive an apology and financial reparations. It came as a surprise to me that in many cases, it has been the apology that gives the most profound lasting impact."

Walter shifted in his seat and placed a hand on top of Melissa's.

"It is completely up to you whether or not you want to participate in this. If you don't, you can decide not to attend the meeting. The mediator understood when I set this up, that I hadn't yet discussed it with you. I'm sorry if I'm putting you on the spot, though you have a little time to make a decision because they aren't scheduled to be here until 12:30. I would have liked to have given you more time, but I thought it would be good for him to see you here, working and sometimes struggling to earn a living. So I was talking with your boss about setting this up at the restaurant when the Assistant States Attorney called, and it needed to be either today or the week after next, so I chose today. And to some extent, I thought it would be better if you didn't have too much time to agonize over it.

"You take a few minutes to think about it. I'm going to let the hostess know who it is that will be joining us, and see if I can round up our waiter or waitress. I have an appetizer coupon that's burning a hole in my pocket, and I just might use it as an appetizer instead of a meal for a change."

When Walter returned to the table, he did his best to relieve Melissa's anxiety by telling stories of clients who passed through his father's law office.

When Nick and Sylvia arrived, the focus of the session shifted. Sylvia had been through this process many times, and worked to keep
the tone friendly and the conversation focused.

Walter felt some empathy for the young man with the off-kilter crew cut and beefy face as he squirmed in his seat and poked at his french fries.

Despite being urged by the woman lawyer to meet Melissa's

eyes, Nick stared down at his plate. "I guess I thought you was just some rich person with a nice apartment. I didn't plan to do it. I was just bumping around the hallway after seeing this guy I knew in the building. When I pushed against your door, it kinda gave way a bit, so I figured I'd bang it harder and see what happened. When it broke open, I started to run away. But no one came out, so I went back in to see what I could find."

Nick raised his head a few degrees, but quickly returned his gaze to the french fries under the intense focus of the group sitting at the table.

"I didn't think about how important this stuff was to her ... um to you. I just took what I could, and when I saw the keys, I figured the car would help me get the stuff away."

He shook his head slowly. "Once I got home, I started worrying about getting caught, so I sold it all to this guy I know who knows a bunch of people. I just didn't think about the car."

After a half minute of silence, Sylvia Gulbranson spoke. "Is there something you want to say directly to Melissa, like we talked about?"

Nick bit his lower lip, and turned his head to face Melissa, though he kept his eyelids lowered. "I'm really sorry for what I did, and I want to do what I can to make it up to you."

Nick muttered a few more words, which Walter didn't catch clearly,
but it was clear from the plaintive look the young man was directing at the county mediator that he was asking "Please, can we go now?"

Walter watched the backs of Sylvia Gulbranson and Nick Black disappear past the hostess stand. Stacking the dishes from that side of the table into a pile by the edge, he slid around into the other side of the booth across from Melissa.

Reaching across the table, he pulled his water glass in front of him and raised it to his lips.

Melissa lifted her head from staring at the collection of sweeteners in their white plastic cradle. "Wow. I mean, wow. Thanks so much for setting this up." She pushed the hair away from her neck and tossed it behind her shoulder. "I wasn't sure if I wanted to do this. I thought that I might be really angry to meet him, or else afraid that the feeling of having my space violated would carry over into other aspects of my life, like here at work. It was tough, and as we sat here, I felt angry and I felt victimized." Melissa took the tissue from her hand, unwrapped it, and blew her nose. "And some of the time, I felt like I could just slug the guy for being stupid and selfish. As we talked, I started to get the feeling that he really did understand what he had put me through, and I think that was definitely some remorse. So, I'm glad I decided to go through with it because I thought that since you had set it up, then it would be a good thing to do."

She reached across the table, twined her fingers around Walter's hand, and gave it a squeeze. "Somehow, it seems like you may know better than I do what's good for me."

Walter studied her face as a small smile pulled up the corners of his lips. "So you think that you'll be able to work out a schedule with Sylvia and Nick?"

Melissa retracted her hand back and scratched her chin. "It's been quite the day, and this has been a lot to absorb. It sounds like he can get me money for a replacement laptop and iPod right away, with the money he got from selling all my stuff. And then he'll try to get another job and pay me something each month. So that's something."

A small tear escaped from her eye, and she brushed it away with the back of her hand. "None of it is going to bring back my grandmother's coat or the suitcase. And I still feel creeped out that someone could just barge into my house and pick through my stuff."

Melissa raised her head to look directly at Nick. "But I do feel a little bad for Nick, so I don't see a need to punish him a lot. It seems like he really does regret stealing my stuff, and I can see how paying it back over a period of time will help remind him of the consequences of acting on impulse. So in short, yes, I think we can work it out."

She gave a sheepish grin. "I'm even thinking about asking the manager if they would give him a job as dishwasher." She lowered her eyes, and then looked up at Walter. "That's weird, isn't it? That I'd want to work with him in the same place after he stole my stuff?"

She shook her head, a strand of hair breaking loose from behind her ears. "I'm just thinking that if it was my kid brother who had messed up, I'd want someone to be willing to give him a break rather than going out for blood."

Walter wrapped his hands around his glass of water. "No, it's not that strange. It may could be viewed as recompense to make him clean up after you for a change." Walter's smile stopped at his lips, as he returned his focus to the topic at hand. "I think it's part of this program that you both see each other as a person who is not that different from yourself, and I think you've embraced that attitude just like you embrace so much of life."

Seeing the intensity in her eyes, Walter looked away and picked up his glass of water and took a sip. When he set it down, he saw the same look gazing over at him. Sliding the appetizer coupon back into his pocket, he reached over for the menu tucked into the side of the booth. Looking straight back into Melissa's eyes, Walter inquired "Could I interest you in sharing a little dessert?"

Infinite Monkeys

EAGLES

by Lloyd J. Rakosnik

The men sat in the boat on the Chippewa Flowage. It was fall
and they were after the big fish. The females would be moving
now. It was that time of the year. They'd be getting in their last
feed before they slowed down for the winter. Getting in the last
bit of fat to make their lives easier during the long dark of the
cool and cold period. Everything would slow down now on the
flowage. The trees would turn. Their leaves becoming different
shades of bright scarlet, tan, gold, and brown.

The trees were mostly hardwoods up here. The leaves would
fall and the ground would be covered in color for a while. Then
the wind would stack and dry the leaves in vast windrows. They
would lose their brightness and turn brown. Then the snows and
thaws and the rains and sun would reduce them to a thick wet
mulch that went back up into the trees to feed them all over again.

The men were tired. Not weary, but content, they had been up
since 5:00 AM and on the water since 5:30. It was late in the
morning now and they put down their rods to get a bite to eat.
Each rod was tied to the boat by nylon cord. All had seen a rod

disappear over the side of a boat or off of a dock when attention wandered. This was cheap insurance.

The Old Guy unwrapped corned beef sandwiches for himself and the others.

Not the stuff you could buy in the stores, which he couldn't stand, but the beef he made for himself. He slow cooked it for hours like his aunt had taught him. There was no fat on the sandwiches he had made the night before. He had cut that away and sliced the beef paper thin and stacked it on rye bread. His rye bread had to have crust. Hard sharp ridges that melted eventually to the steady chewing of teeth leaving the tangy sweet-sour taste he loved so much on his tongue.

His beef required that. He said so himself. They passed the sandwiches around the three of them.

They sat there looking around at the water, the sky, the air. They talked, but not too much. They enjoyed the silence they shared together, not having to talk, knowing that they were all OK with that.

They were fishing with suckers. The big fish liked big food at this time of year. So they had one pound suckers on the line. Each fish was rigged with razor sharp treble hooks. Hooks designed to drive deep into the jaw of the big fish and never let go. All the leaders were steel. The teeth of the musky would slash through any nylon with barely a shake of their head. The new woven lines were a little better but still no match for the teeth of the fish. Steel had its place out here. So the leaders were steel and the lines were woven from kevlar. A twenty pound test woven line was the thickness of a six pound piece of monofilament. The old man thought that was a great idea. This line would be almost indiscernible once it was in the water. Yes this was a great development. It wouldn't stretch in the water and with the narrow diameter it would cut the water better conveying more information to his hands. This would work out fine. Just fine.

The suckers were all rigged the same way. One barb of the treble hook was delicately inserted into the back right in front of the dorsal fin in line with the spine. The scales were gently pushed aside and the steel pushed into place. The other two hooks sat exposed and in line with the body of the fish. It could swim easily like this and any predator that took this bait would get hooked. The fish swam near the surface. All three baits were within five yards of each other. They formed a small loose school.

The Old Man sat in the bow. He leaned forward and took a beer offered to him.

His friend pointed; he was the youngster, Dan - barely 51 years old. "Look, eagles, they're after the suckers." He laughed. The bait was effective from above and from below.

The driver, Ben, looked up too. "Yep, they think that is a free lunch."

They watched the large birds ride the currents and circle up in the sky. They all could tell they were eagles since their wings had a straight leading edge. Hawks and falcons had bent wings and besides nothing but an eagle was that big.

Thirty yards behind the boat a sucker floated on its side fluttering its' tail as it died on the surface while swimming in a perfect seven-foot circle. In the water the invisible line floated over itself making a perfect loop that wavered and danced just below the surface of the water.

Twenty-three hundred feet up in the air, with its six-foot wings catching the air currents perfectly, the eagle saw the fish flutter as it died. The air and wings held the eagle suspended for several seconds. Then he went to get dinner. He came down very fast. Maybe the men could have done something if he had come right at the fish; as it was he came down about fifty yards away from the sucker. Then just feet above the surface of the lake he planed out hurtling towards the fish. His attack was perfect, honed by both instinct and practice it carried him right to his quarry, and placed the bait right in his talons. As he lifted into the air it placed a bracelet of looped fishing line around his legs. As he gained air the line tightened and now he was fairly and truly caught. The bird lifted itself and its' prey into the air first with the desire to find a safe perch to eat at and then with an increasing fury to escape the line tightening around its' feet. The great wings cupped air and powered the predator aloft. Below the line hissed as it was snapped out of the water at an increasingly fast pace.

The rod tip arced up and the drag on the reel worked perfectly.

Dan was in the middle of the boat with a beer in one hand and a sandwich in the other as the seven foot musky rod spun around turning itself into a graphite buggy whip that caught him right across the side of his face. The sound of the blow was like a mallet hitting raw meat.

"Damn!" was all that came out of his mouth as he crumpled in the boat dropping beer and sandwich to grab his face.

The Old Guy grabbed the rod in self-defense while Ben went for Dan. Ben pulled Dan's hands away from his face to see the damage. There wasn't any blood and the orbit of the eye seemed OK but there was bruising already and it had been a hell of a shot to take. Especially since he had no idea that it was coming.

"We'd best head in" Ben said.

"Can't yet", the Old Guy said, "we've still got the bird. We have to get him down to get the line off of him. It could kill him."

"I'm OK," Dan said. "Land the bird and let's go in then. I'm swollen but I can still see with both eyes and it doesn't feel as if anything is broken. So I'm OK for a while."

The Old Guy started in on the Eagle. He played him like a fish but in reverse. The rod was meant to bend the other way but this didn't matter much once he began to get the hang of it. He signaled Ben to move towards the center of the lake so the bird would have to pick the boat for his final perch before it was too exhausted to fight anymore.

The fight lasted a good seven or eight minutes before the eagle perched on the bows of the boat.

The Old Guy whistled through his teeth. "Would you look at that! He's got to be three feet tall. Take a quick photo of him before we get that line off of him so we can have proof of this fish story."

They took the shots quickly while commenting on their luck since the eagle did not seem to be hooked. He seemed quiet for the time being. He would try to lift a leg and shake it then bend his head toward the leg as if he wanted to pluck at something that bothered him. The sucker dangled from the line around his leg. It was forgotten now.

It was his quietness that made them make the mistake.

The Old Guy sat still for a minute then snapped out his big bullet knife. The Remington resided in his hip pocket. It was flat enough that he could sit on it without discomfort. He kept a rawhide lanyard on it so he could get it out of his pocket fast. He kept the blade razor sharp. He passed the rod back to Dan butt first.

"Whatca' doin'?" Dan asked taking the rod.

"Yeah" said Ben "What's up? You going to kill that bird?"

"I'm going to cut the line around his legs to let him go. He'll just take off. Then we can go in or keep on fishing here. Whatever you want to do."

The Old Guy eased up on the eagle closing the distance quietly and slowly. He didn't look directly at the bird. He kept his eyes down. No sense in spooking the animal when it would be free soon. As he closed on the bird it sidestepped on the gunwale to keep some distance between them. He was close enough now to reach the leg where the line was looped. He could smell the animal odor of the bird. His arm stretched out in front of the great talons. The tip of the knife slid up between the legs catching the tough line that held the eagle captive. He could see the single loop. There didn't look to be any damage to the legs of eagle. It hadn't cut into the legs yet.

Ben and Dan heard the quiet ping of the knife blade as it cut through the line.

Dan and Ben saw the Old Guy smile as the line parted.

Ben and Dan both saw the eagle hop forward and sink its talons into the Old Guy's arm. He perched there as if he were on a tree limb.

The heart attack ripped through him so fast he couldn't tell which hurt more, his left arm for what was happening in his body or his right arm where the bird perched gripping tightly. He was no good with his left hand. He never had been. He was a righty from childhood up to the present. He wanted to hang onto something with his left. He wanted to hold himself up.

He moved his arm a little and the bird ratcheted his talons down crushing the life out of its prey.

"Prey," he thought, "damn he thinks he has a rabbit or a snake or some meal. If I'm quiet he'll let go and be on his way".

The eagle ratcheted down again crushing the meat in his arm. The true pain hit him then.

The radius and ulna were grinding together; flexing under the unrelenting pressure. Spit flew from the Old Guy's mouth as he gasped. He was sweating heavily now. His breath shortened. "Chest" he muttered, "chest" as he twisted against the pain that racked him.

Ben came up with the Colt Match Target Woodsman working the slide on the pistol expertly. "I can hit him clean he said. We disjoint the feet to get him off and get you to a doc."

"The hell you say, leave the bird alone. No killing. He's on my arm. I don't want him dead. Put the Colt back in the canvas holster and leave it in my tackle box."

"How long can you put up with that bird?" Dan asked. He

looked to the shore. "We can drive in maybe." His face was starting to swell and turn purple.

The eagle hooded, spreading his wings to cover his "kill" and claim it as his own. He glared out of his yellow eyes, seeming to stare them down. He kee-kecked loudly and raucously.

"I know that they can be made to move if approached in the right way" Ben said. "I just forget how to make them move. It's a simple thing to do."

"Look at his hand, Ben, look at his hand!" Dan was pointing. The right hand was swollen and dark purple. The fingers had contracted into a claw that rested on the boat seat. The big Remington had slipped into the bottom of the boat.

The Old Guy wanted that back. The knife was important; he had had it a long time. It was a good knife. He tried to get it with his left hand but it was too far. "Later," he thought, "I'll get it later."

The eagle extended his neck reaching down with his bill, cocking his head to one side as if checking on something. Then he increased his grip. The Old Guy's bones cracked. "Kee-Riste" came from his clenched teeth.

He slumped backwards, forgetting the knife, and saw his daughter. He knew this was a hallucination. He didn't know why she was there. He recalled the camping trip when she was a little girl. Blond curls all over her head, running away from the car, happy as can be, a sharp hatchet in her hands. She had taken it off of the tailgate where he had laid it. She ran up to a slender tree with gleaming eyes and swung the hand ax against the trunk. There was a gentle tap-tap-tap that made him turn his head. In a breath he was racing to get to the child. He didn't give a damn about the tree, all he could see was the possibility of blood gushing from a slashed arm or leg. He spanked her because he was angry with himself for leaving the ax where she could get to it. It scared him, the damage she could have done to herself. He hated the emotion of fear and since she had evoked it in him he lashed out at her. He hit her. Not in the face or with his fist or even more than once but he knew he was wrong. It wasn't that kids shouldn't get spankings but they had to deserve it before they got a whippin'. Funny thing was he never picked his hand up to that girl before that or ever again afterwards. He might threaten to do something but he never could.

He hated the position he was in. Laying back as if he was resting. He hated it because it looked sloppy. He looked sprawled out. It looked like he didn't care. Like he had given up. He couldn't stand that. He sat up a bit, moving his shoulders forward. He sat up like a man. He kept his arm still and tried to think. It came to him that he had killed too many deer. He shook his head to clear it.

This was nuts. He was hallucinating again from the pain. He remembered standing on the moraine with his brother fifty years ago, an ancient lever action in his hands. He had made the cartridges himself, pressing in a new primer, pouring in the right amount of powder, seating the big lead bullets and then crimping them so they would fire and fly straight and true. The gun looked new but it was almost one hundred years old then. The deer had run right up to them. He was standing still with the air moving into his face. He had put them in the perfect spot. He didn't move and the deer couldn't see him. The two does knew that something was wrong but couldn't tell what it was. They stood there testing the wind, searching with their eyes for the danger they could not see fifteen feet in front of them. Their feet were covered in the oak leaves they were searching for mast – the fallen acorns they so loved to eat.

"They're does," his brother whispered.

He looked down the sights of the rifle. The butt of the gun hard against his shoulder. The gun light as a feather balanced in his hands. Both of his eyes open as looked past the deer it front of him.

"I'm waiting for the buck," he whispered back. He saw it then. Sneaking along with its head near to the ground. Moving from windfalls, to bushes, and then to brush piles to stay hidden as much as possible. He waited. Patient in his knowledge of what the gun could do. Knowing that the 255 grain lead slug couldn't bust through brush, that he had to have a clear shot at the head or the chest area. He knew that the big bullet had plenty of slap, plenty of smash to do what he wanted it to do.

He looked at the eye of the buck. He could see the eye. It was brown as fresh brewed coffee. It's where he shot the deer. He hung the fine ivory bead of the front sight just below that eye. He marveled at the clarity of the colors. The ivory white of the sight and the coffee brown of the eye were never more vibrant and alive. He covered the eye with the fine white of the ivory; then he let out half of his breath, and squeezed the trigger. He didn't hear the shot or feel the recoil. His left hand supported the gun while his right ripped the lever down and slammed it back up just like he practiced hundreds of times. He had a new round in the chamber and could go again if need be. He never took his eyes off of the animal after he shot. He watched it go nose first into the ground. Dead before it hit the ground. Just like he had planned it. He knew it was dead but he went to high port arms out of habit. It was a safe way to hold a gun and one that kept it ready.

The second shot whipped his head around to the right. His brother had killed a second, larger buck that had been behind the first. He had never seen it back there. Both were within thirty yards of where they stood.

The does bleated and seemed to shrink down until their bellies almost touched the earth as they finally decided they were near danger and streaked away. It was a good day. They had both filled their tags. The sun was never brighter. The sky was never more blue. The scent of the powder hung in the air. The octagon barrel was warm to the touch. They dressed out the deer cutting swiftly and surely. They slung the rifles across their backs and dragged the dear out by their antlers leaving a clear path in the leaves.

They had been strong then. Now, time had played tricks with their arms and lungs. Their legs and their eyes were not what they should be. They could not do that again.

He shook himself to clear his head. He had to stay in the here and now to get through this. He saw the boat and his friends clearly. He knew he was old now. He was no longer hunting; his daughters were grown up, safely through college, and tucked into good careers. He didn't have to worry about them going off to war. He needed to remember where he was now, not what had been.

"You need help," Dan said. "We need to get that eagle off of your arm. We have to do it."

Ben came forward into the middle of the boat. "That animal has to come off your arm. You'll lose that arm if this goes on."

"I'll take an oar and carefully come up behind this big fellow.

You lift him a bit and I'll slide the oar up behind him. I won't touch his tail; I'll be careful of that. Then I'll just touch the round shaft of the oar to the back of his feet. He should step backwards onto the oar" Ben told the Old Guy.

"Let me know when you are ready," Ben said. He worked his way towards the bows. The eagle watched him with golden eyes. Ben looked at the bird, then at Dan, and last at the Old Guy; "Lift your arm and hold it steady," he said.

His arm came up and remained steady for just long enough. Ben slipped the oar behind the eagle touching the back of its claws. It rotated its head and then stepped backwards onto the oar. It kek-keked snapping its beak in irritation.

Dan grabbed the Old Guy by the shirt front pulling him away from the bird and towards the stern. He let him slump down onto the boat bottom. Then he picked up the dip net and waved it at the eagle. The eagle screamed and leapt into the air circling the boat. They watched it climb high into the air.

Spotting the big Remington in the bottom of the boat Ben picked it up. He closed it. He looked at the bone handle with the inlaid brass cartridge, then he tucked it into the Old Guy's hip pocket. It belonged there.

Ben started the boat. They went in together. The father and his sons. They took him to the hospital where he was treated and kept until it was safe for him to go home. He hated it there but he endured it. When his chest was healed and he could use his arm again he left there. He went home to his house and his dog. He lived for more years and he shot doves at the end of August, pheasants in November, and went fishing again in the fall. He always loved eagles.

A DAY IN THE LIFE

By Tom Ostler

The fire truck rumbled and swayed as it snaked through the frozen traffic on its way to the latest emergency. It lurched headlong into a swirling envelope of smoke and steam with its sirens and clanging bells suffocating all other sound. Strapped safely within the cocoon of the cab sat Ben Anstett, poised to leap into action the instant the massive machine came to a stop. The wailing siren, rising and falling through the octaves, beat on him incessantly as if someone had taken a jackhammer to his stomach. When the big truck finally squealed to a stop Ben found himself paralyzed with inaction—time seemed to unravel as his mind fought to cut through the haze; to make order out of chaos. Slowly, as if his body knew before he did, the realization that the siren was just his cell phone buzzing somewhere across the darkened room jolted Ben awake. The fire was a recurring dream since childhood—an example of where his mind could take him if he wasn't vigilant.

The room was nearly pitch black and wholly unfamiliar. Even the fading sound of his cell phones ring felt disorienting and off-kilter. This was not his home. It was a spare bedroom in his sister's house. Ben had been staying here for the past few weeks and had yet to feel at ease in this tiny room. He felt downright uncomfortable anywhere else in Christy's house.

Sitting up in bed, Ben waited until he fully understood where he was and what had just happened. The dream had seemed so real he could almost taste the smoke and ash. In it he had naturally accepted that he was a fireman, when in reality he had never set foot in a fire station. The ringing cell phone invaded his REM sleep and became the catalyst for the dream. What was he dreaming before the fire? He thought for a moment but nothing came to mind. It was rare when Ben could remember his dreams and it usually took an abrupt awaking such as this to remember even the smallest fragment. A few minutes passed before he transitioned back to reality. In the faint light he saw the outline of the window and the perpetual halo from the street light peeking through the curtains. To his left, through the adjoining bathroom door, he could see the small green indicator light glowing full power on his electric toothbrush. There on his right, at the foot of the dresser, was his cell phone blinking innocently after it had vibrated itself off the dresser and onto the floor.

Ben was a cop, not a beat cop, but a detective and this was his cop phone. If it went off it meant that something serious had happened and worth the effort to climb out of bed to hear the message. "Ben, this is Robin, give me a call as soon as you get this message…it's important." The time stamp read 2:53 am. Robin was Ben's partner and the two of them had just ended an 18-hour shift at midnight and parted company—he to his sister's spare room and Robin to her apartment. Ben hit Robin's speed dial. She picked up on the first ring and spoke before he could utter a sound. "Ben, Lisa was involved in a hit-and-run tonight. You better get over to Mother Teresa's ASAP."

Ben said nothing and hung up the phone. Robin had been his partner for only two months and he was just now beginning to interpret the nuances in her voice. She was holding something back despite the gravity of what she said. Ben put on the same rumpled suit he had climbed out of only a few hours ago and slipped out of the house. His only witness was Max the tabby who watched with disinterest from atop the dresser as Ben hurried out the door.

The eastern horizon had yet to hint of the hot steamy dawn that would arrive in a few hours time. Every sound he made echoed off the suburban stillness like a waiter dropping a dish in a quiet restaurant. Ben drove without the radio as he sped to the hospital, focusing on keeping his thoughts in order. Every stop light was an eternity; mostly he cautiously ignored them and zipped through knowing he could flash his badge if any rookie cop was foolish enough to stop him. He instinctively knew to park near the Emergency Room, in the spaces reserved for official police business. Robin was waiting for him on the curb.

Before Ben could ask any question, Robin raised her hand to stop him and said in a soft, low voice, "I got a call from the sheriff's department around 2:30. At 11 o'clock last night some drunk hit a bunch of parked cars on Drury, 7 cars at least over a 3-block stretch. One of the cars he hit was Lisa's SUV, apparently, just as she was getting in. The impact pinned her between a mailbox and her car. By the time the paramedics arrived, it was too late." Robin dropped her eyes, "I'm sorry, Ben."

"Where is she now?" He said in a deep authoritarian tenor. He didn't realize it, but Ben used his "command voice", the voice cops are trained to use when they mean business—when they're in charge of a situation. Thinking through all the possible scenarios as he drove over, he had avoided the possibility of

Lisa's death as being too ghoulish to contemplate. This news collapsed any glimmer of hope he had as easily as if it were a house of cards.

The two of them walked through the fluorescent glare of the Emergency Room then deep into the quiet labyrinth of corridors, turning this way and that, approaching a goal neither one of them wanted to reach. The hallways lost the welcoming façade as they made their way into the staff-only section of the building. The overhead lights dimmed to a somber tone, which matched Ben's spirits. Eventually they arrived at a non-descript door marked "Private, Morgue Viewing Room, No. 1."

"I'll be outside." Robin whispered, as she stepped aside and let Ben enter alone. Inside the room were a single chair and a gurney. Upon that gurney lay the still form of Lisa Anstett.

Ben had been around enough bodies not to be shocked by what he saw. After twenty years on the force he had seen every conceivable cause of death and before that he had been with the Marines in Beirut on that awful day suicide bombers attacked the barracks. He had learned the hard way that a night of drinking, trying to forget, actually brought back the memories of screams, colors and smells that could only be described as horrific. He learned to take his feelings, encase them in cement, and sink them deep into the pool of his soul. His instinctive reaction was to do that now. It was the only way he knew to survive this tragedy.

Above, he could hear the slight hum of the fluorescent lights and the whisper of the air system as it pumped cool air into the room. Lisa lay under a white sheet, her head and face exposed. Had this been anywhere else he would have thought she were sleeping. He had no desire to examine her body; there was a particular revulsion to that act. He sat down next to her and reached under the sheet to take her left hand. He pushed out of his mind the sensation that he was no longer holding anything living and willed himself to hold his wife's hand. It was soft and cold and turned easily as he brought it up to his lips to kiss. Lisa's nails were freshly done, as she usually had them, and on her third finger were her engagement and wedding rings.

"I don't feel married anymore," Lisa said over the silent breakfast table a month ago. "I mean Ben, what's the point? What am I getting out of all this?"

Ben could feel the blood in his veins turn to ice at the tone of Lisa's voice. They had been over this territory time and time before. Jaded, he knew that this morning was going to be lost in endless conversation, but he also knew at some level Lisa had a point.

"Honey, I know it's been tough on you. I'm doing my best." was all he could say knowing that he had said the same words a thousand times. The result would also be the same. Tears, hurt feelings, and eventually a silent understanding that, over time, a thaw would come and things would return to the truce each of them tolerated.

"We've been through this before Lisa. Being a cop…"

Lisa interrupted. "Spare me the speech, Ben. I know it isn't easy, but it seems like you've quit trying. You've built up such a wall no one can get in and you can't get out. When Larry retired you said it was no big deal—getting a new partner, it happens all the time." Lisa got up and mechanically went through the motion of cleaning the kitchen just to keep her hands busy. "I watched you. You were nervous as a kitten for a full week before you teamed up with Robin."

"No I wasn't."

"That's BS and you know it, Ben! You actually tossed and turned all week. I watched you tense up, just as much as you are now." Lisa paused at the sink and sighed. "The worst part was you didn't reach out to me. Here it is a month now with your new partner and you haven't lightened up one iota." Lisa looked at Ben, still sitting at the table with an all too familiar lost expression on his face.

"Megan needs you. She needs a father, not simply some guy living in the same house and I need you, Ben. I swear, if we had a dog, you'd show it more affection than you do Meg or me." Ben was happy Megan wasn't around to listen to this conversation—again. She was next door with the Franklin twins, having one of their frequent sleepovers.

Ben knew this was his cue to respond, to make things better with words or better still with actions, yet all he could do was fumble with both. "Lisa, I don't know what to say other than I'm doing my best. I think you know that. I'm just not built that way; no cop is—to be the touchy-feely guy you want." His words were inadequate because he wasn't able to access his feelings and articulate them. All he ended up doing was looking stunned in front of his plate of pancakes.

"Ben, I need a break. I don't know if I want to be a cop's wife anymore. I don't know if I want to be your wife anymore. I just don't feel I'm really living—too much is on hold for me." Ben tried to answer her again. The words came out all jumbled and awkward so he began to repeat himself. "I'm doing my best Lisa." was the only coherent sentence he could utter.

Lisa stopped his weak response with a sharp look and said "Stop! Stop it, Ben. I'm taking Megan and spending the week in Kansas City with my parents. I'd like it very much if you would find a place to live before we get back." With that she slid her rings off, placed them on the table, and walked out the door.

That was a six weeks ago and in the interim they had had dinner several times. Ben had even spent a weekend with Lisa. Things were looking promising as they had talked of reconciling. Now, on the cusp of his life turning around for the better, this had to happen. The only bright spot, if there was one, was that in all the time they were separated Ben had never seen Lisa wear her wedding ring, and here it was. It was such a beautiful act of hope on her part that it made the reality of his loss feel like falling off a cliff. He kissed the palm of her hand, the way she liked it most and drank in the fading aroma of her perfume. Standing, he looked down upon her serene face and kissed her on her forehead, then her lips with a gentleness he wasn't aware he possessed. He stood there adrift in a sea of loss, incapable of moving or thinking. Like a faucet with a drip filling a basin, his sadness grew deeper with each passing heartbeat.

"Where's the driver?" Ben mournfully asked as he entered the corridor.

"He's being held by the sheriff's department. They're not going to let you near him, you know that." Robin sounded as weary as she looked. For the first time since they partnered up, Ben could see the years on her face.

"I just want to see him, Blake. To see what kind of man could do this." He always called Robin by her last name—it was one of the ways he kept her distant.

183

Robin sized him up for a few moments, as if reading his mind. Then with an understanding all her own, she gave Ben a nod and the two walked out into the pre-dawn air.

As a courtesy, the Sheriff's police allowed neighboring police department officers into their holding area to observe interrogations. The interview room the driver was held in was as sterile as the one in which he'd left Lisa. At one end of an aluminum table sat a rumpled looking man in his late 30's, thin, pale complexion, unusually well groomed despite recent events. "Some suburban golfer type." Ben told himself. On the other side of the table were two empty chairs.

A moment later, a Sheriff's deputy walked past them without acknowledgement and entered the room. He sat across from the driver and began talking as he flipped through a folder. Ben watched the driver intently as the deputy was undoubtedly telling him what damage he had done, leaving the scene of an accident and causing the death of an innocent bystander. At first, the expression on the drivers face was uninterested and blank. As the deputy continued building his case in an obvious effort to overwhelm him, the driver did something unexpected. He became indignant, gesturing as if he were the injured party. In fact, he appeared to be self-righteous and acting as if he were the victim. Ben just knew in the core of his being that the driver must have one hell of a lawyer and no matter what he had done earlier in the evening, there wasn't one shred of guilt within him.

"Blake, do you see this guy?!" Ben asked.

"I see him, Ben." she said flatly.

"This asshole believes he's going to get away with this." Ben's voice was rising in intensity; in a way mimicking the driver's own reaction behind the bulletproof glass.

The absurdity of this cosmic joke made Ben chuckle, "Some $700 an hour lawyer is going to waltz in here and snatch him away and the closest thing to justice he's ever going to see is a TV show." In the briefest of thoughts Ben regretted surrendering his pistol as protocol demanded. A snapshot image filled his mind of emptying a magazine into the chest of the driver. Even before this image could register as a thought, Ben snapped back to reality and sank lower into his grief.

Robin watched Ben deflate like a balloon in front of her. "Come on Ben, you need to head home. It's almost 7 am and Megan is going to return from her sleep-over to an empty house." With the thought of his daughter for the first time, Ben collapsed against the wall embarrassed by his selfishness in thinking Lisa's death only affected him.

"Take me home, Robin." Ben said almost inaudibly. They both were silent on the drive home. Ben staring out the passenger window, wondering how the world pretended to be the same with a veneer so thin that the slightest breeze would tear it apart to reveal the ugly truth and pain only he knew.

"I hate this guy, Blake. " Ben said as he watched a toddler on a big wheel zip down the sidewalk followed by an attentive Mom.

"We were on our way to patching things up, Lisa and I. Did I tell you that?" Ben glanced over at Robin and she gave him a quick look as they negotiated a corner. "Now that's all gone. Did you see how arrogant he was? He crushed her life as easily as stepping on an ant." Ben took a deep breath, exhaling nothingness, breathing in a building rage within him. Again he imagined standing over the lifeless body of the driver—steaming bullet holes in his chest wafting retribution with satisfaction flooding Ben's awakening mind as the only antidote to his grief.

"Turn around, Blake I'm going to kill that son of a bitch!" Ben tapped Robin on the arm to get her attention to follow his order.

"Sorry, Ben, that's not going to happen," she said casually, eyes fixed on the road. "It's not about him anymore, don't you understand that? His fate is out of your hands."

"Bullshit!" he shouted back, startling her. "He took her away just as I was getting her back."

Ben was all adrenalin now, just like his first on-foot pursuit as a rookie. He reached into his coat and pulled out his pistol and pointed it at his partner. "Robin." he said in a low, mechanical voice as powerful as the bullet in the chamber. Blood was throbbing in his veins, his heart pounding in his chest.

The instant Robin realized what was happening she slammed on the brakes to a full stop. Ben's gun never wavered from its target.

"You're going to have to use that. I'm not taking you back." Robin said in her command voice. "Do you think killing him or killing me to get to him is going to bring Lisa back? Do you think you can replace your sadness with this rage—that this will ever be enough, ever set things right?" Robin put the car in park letting the traffic behind them figure out for themselves how to deal with this crisis.

"Now put that gun away before you get into real trouble."

"I can't, Blake. I have nothing else, this is who I am, what I am."

She barked back, "That's bullshit, Ben, and you know it." Then softened, "I never told you that Lisa and I talked a few times since you separated." Robin never let her eyes lose contact with his, despite the perspiration that began to drip into her eyes, burning them—she never wavered.

"She was worried about you. She loved you but didn't know how to reach you anymore. She said, 'It's like he's on a boat drifting away from shore, only the current knows where he's going,' She loved you, Ben. She wouldn't want you to be doing this now."

They had caused a pretty good spectacle in the middle of the street with car horns bleating behind them. Both Robin and Ben could sense commotion outside of the car. The police had undoubtedly been called because sirens could now be heard off in the distance, reminding Ben of the urgency of his fire truck dream.

"Ben, this isn't what Lisa would have wanted. Put the gun down, for her sake, for Megan's sake. She needs you now, more than you can imagine."

Seconds passed.

Ben's eyebrows slowly softened and his steely glare faded. The pistol lowered to his lap just seconds before two patrolmen approached the car with their weapons drawn. Robin and Ben slowly fished out and flashed their badges before the patrolmen had a chance to ask what was going on. As the squad pulled away, Robin glanced at Ben, who nodded in reply and the two continued on home, to the waiting Megan.

Ben entered through the kitchen door and checked if Megan was home. Peeking into her room Ben saw that the bed hadn't been slept in. "Good," he thought, "Megan must still be next door." He headed into the living room and crumpled onto the couch for an agonizing wait. Lisa's presence was still alive in this house and the ache Ben felt knowing she would never return to the home she had made for Megan and him weighed down upon him and nearly crushed him. Just as fatigue got the better of him, Megan exploded into the room and jolted him to attention.

"Dad! I didn't expect to see you here. Mom must still be asleep, 'cause she's not in the kitchen."

"She's not here, Meg."

Megan gave her dad a quizzical look, not comprehending, but based on the pained expressing on his face, something had to be wrong—horribly wrong.

"Dad?"

"Sit down, Meg. I've some bad news for you, for us all." Megan sat down in the chair opposite her dad, her gaze fixed on him. Her body was tense waiting to receive the blow.

"Is it Mom?" Megan guessed. When his eyes welled up and tears appeared on his cheeks she had her answer.

"When? How?" she whispered.

"Last night. Your mom was climbing into her car when it was hit by a drunk driver. She got caught in the open driver door when the accident happened—broken back they tell me. She never knew what hit her." There, the worst of it was out. Ben slowly raised his eyes from the carpet to his daughter, afraid to make even the briefest of eye contact. Megan didn't move for a minute. Her gaze fixed laser-like upon her father and Ben shrank back from his daughter's gaze without moving a muscle.

"Dad?" she pleaded.

"Meg, that's all I know."

Ben leaned forward and reached out for her. Megan began to put the pieces together. Like a series of dominos, each event that led to this moment had a predecessor. In her mind's eye, the very first domino, the catalyst, was her father and his inability to love her mom.

"No, Dad! This is all your fault. She wouldn't have been out with her girl friends if you were home, if you were a better husband!" Megan shouted in a hysterical voice at the top of her lungs.

"Even when you were here, you were in your own little world, 'decompressing' you called it; Mom called it running away, being vacant." Megan rose from her chair, her energy rising, swirling around her like a dust storm.

"Meg, it wasn't like that."

"No, Dad!" she said with conviction, "it was even worse. You'd have your head buried in the TV and I could hear Mom crying in the bedroom. You were too thick to see what you were doing to her. She was suffocating, that's what she called it, and finally, finally, she threw you out of the house. These past couple of weeks were her happiest—and mine too!"

189

Driving in the last nail, Megan stepped closer and glowered over her father, "Mom hated you, and so do I. I hate you!" With that she ran down the hall, barricading herself in her bedroom.

Ben sat there wanting desperately to follow his daughter to exonerate himself, but no words came. The silence was thick and his thoughts collapsed inward upon themselves until neither his body nor his mind would function.

An hour passed. Outside the world continued taking no notice of the emptiness and sorrow under this roof. Sounds of life crept into the silent house; birds chirped, dogs barked, children laughed and cried and in spite of the undeniable presence of life outside, Ben had ceased to live. He sat there, as if cast in bronze, without a thought in his head, only the image of Megan sprawled across her bed sobbing for her loss or snarling in her anger toward him reached his consciousness. Not knowing what he would do when he got there, Ben dragged himself down the hall to Megan's bedroom. In front of her room he slid to the floor, resting against the door jam with his feet sprawled into the open door of the master bedroom. Megan's sobs could be heard through the heavy bedroom door.

"Megan? I don't know if you can hear me or even want to listen to me." 'Where to go from here?' Ben thought. He was fighting a weariness that smothered his feelings, yet alone his ability to articulate them. He was tumbling again, into the chasm that lay between he and Lisa, and now, he and Megan.

"I don't blame you for hating me. I know that it must look like I drove your mom away, as if I put her into that car last night or pointed that drunk driver at her." Ben paused and took a pained breath. "I was angry at myself for pushing your mom away. I dug myself into a hole and I didn't know how to get out. I was paralyzed in..." Ben searched for the feeling. What was the emotion? How to put a label on something that Ben didn't fully comprehend? How to communicate any of this to Megan?

"I guess it was fear, Megan. I didn't know it at the time, perhaps I don't even know today what it really was, but I was paralyzed whenever I got away from what I knew best. I loved your mom every day, ever since the day we met; only I didn't know how to build a bridge to her. I felt awkward and shy and at times stupid whenever we got close to talking about the things that mattered to her. It was so far removed from what I knew that it was tough for me to switch...worlds."

Ben was talking to the ghost of Lisa as much as he was talking to Megan. "Ever since high school I had to forge my own way, to develop a thick hide that protected me. When grandpa died, Grandma and I never talked about how we felt. We, I, didn't know how. I guess we were both hurt, and sad and lonely, but neither one of us knew how to break out of the silent way we dealt with each other. That's the pattern I got into with your mom. I wanted to change, I just didn't know how."

Ben listened for any sign of life coming from Megan's room. There was no sound in the house other than the sound of his breathing.

"I'm more scared now than I was yesterday, Megs, I don't know what to do. I've lost your mom and I don't know what I'd do if I lost you too." Ben choked on that thought. Perhaps he had already lost his daughter's love by being a distant, cold-hearted father and the thought that he had hurt her the same way he had hurt Lisa was unbearable.

The wall, that barbed-wire fence that had been constructed over a lifetime and separated him from the rest of humanity was somewhere else for the moment. Ben began to feel the true depth of his sorrow for the first time. He closed his eyes and fell over into the fetal position. Uncontrollable whimpers attacked his body. He was defenseless against them and almost welcomed them as Job had welcomed all that God had delivered upon him.

"I'm sorry, Lisa" he whispered, "I'm sorry, Megan." He said a bit louder, and then began to softly sob again.

What seemed like an hour later the bedroom door slowly opened and Megan crawled out of her room and into the arms of her father. They both laid there in the fetal position for minutes without talking. Ben enveloped her as if to shield her from the ills of the world. He kissed the back of her head, wrapping her tightly in his arms. Here was his life now, this 14-year-old angel.

"Oh, Megs! I'm so ashamed. I wanted to kill that drunk driver this morning. I was so angry I drew my pistol on my partner. I wanted someone else to pay for what happened and that person was almost you." Sobbing, he spurted out "I don't want you to pay for my mistakes. I want to be a real dad to you, not what I have been."

"I don't hate you, Dad, not really." Megan whispered. "I hate that drunk driver and I wish you had…"

"Hush, Megs, Robin was right, that wouldn't change what happened, it'd only make it worse, especially for you."

"It hurts so much, Dad, I can hardly breathe."

"I feel that too, Megs. I don't know if I have the strength to get up from here, there's so much that has to be done, but all I want to do is hold you, protect you from the world." A pang of doubt hit Ben and he became self conscious of where he was and he started to feel foolish about getting emotional and saying too much. He could feel Megan crying in front of him and he was reminded of how much she sounded like Lisa when he hurt her with his indifference.

"Megs, I know I have flaws, some of them big ones, some of them get in my way of being a good parent. God knows, they got in the way of me being a good husband." Ben's fear had returned but this time it was a different shade. He was no longer afraid of being seen for what he was. He was afraid his heart would burst from the love for his daughter that was cascading within—that was a fear he could embrace.

"Dad? Can we just lay here a while?"

The afternoon came. The afternoon went. Father and daughter held each other in silence.

Infinite Monkeys

TICKETS, PLEASE

by Brian Cable

"I want to redeem these tickets, please," said a decayed man delicately offering a bundle of yellowed tickets to the boy wearing an Infinite Fun Zone uniform with a My Name is: Moron, Apparently nametag.

The boy doesn't look up from his View 2000, which is currently displaying a combination of his favorite TV show (the audio playing into the voice chip in his ear at 20% volume), his girlfriend idling in a coffee shop with her own View 2000, a dynamic transcript of his friends' current drunken conversation around a fire in the woods of Terra III, and Camelot Graffiti Knightz, the latest video game to come out that can be played using only eye movement and featuring autopause, which would pause the game automatically when he looked away from the game, and unpause when he looked back.

"I believe I have 100 of them. 100 precisely," said the old man, trying to elicit a response by being helpful.

Moron taps one of the slots on the Employee EZ Answer Sheet.

"Ticket redemption is automatic. Just take what you are eligible for and the scanner will let you leave," said a voice into the voice chips of everyone in the shop, in a slightly feminine but otherwise neutral voice.

"I tried that, but it stopped me," said the man. "My name is Gary, by the way. What's yours?"

Another tap. "If the scanner stopped you from leaving, you're holding objects worth more than the tickets you have. You are holding items worth -- 95 -- tickets. You are holding -- 0 -- tickets."

"That's not true. They're right here in my hand. Look," said Gary, setting a shaking hand holding the tickets on the counter. "There's obviously more than zero tickets in that pile."

Moron taps another button. "We're sorry you are having problems understanding simple concepts. Please leave and Mindlink your concerns to our corporate office on your way out."

"I'm not leaving," said Gary in a louder voice. "You are going to help me if I have to burn the whole place down with you in it!" Gary turned his body around and faced the couple waiting behind him, who looked startled. "My apologizes. I didn't mean it."

"We understand," said the woman. "Would you like some help with Mr. Moron?"

"I don't know if that's such a good idea, Jenny," said her companion. "Why don't we just take the man's unicorn and use our tickets towards it?"

"Because if we did that, then this stupid big dumb company

wins. And you'll be sleeping on the couch tonight." She sealed her statement with an iron stare.

The man sighed. "Fine. We can talk to him."

"Thanks, but let me handle this myself." Gary turned back to Moron, pulled a small metal object out of his pocket, set the timer to 20 minutes, and tossed it at the View 2000. It quickly snapped to the screen magnetically, which immediately shut its power off.

"Hey, what's the big idea?" yelled Moron, finally speaking. He tried to pry off the device, but without any luck.

"Don't bother trying to take it off. It's childproof, so you don't stand a chance," said Gary. "I bought that MiniEMP for when the kids come over and I need to get their attention. I'm glad it has other uses."

"I was doing some very important work-related stuff on there, you know," said Moron.

"No you weren't. There's nothing more important than the customer anyway, or has that changed since I've been out of the work force?"

"Maybe it has."

Jenny, stomping her foot for effect, said, "You know, you're just the rudest man, Mr. Moron? We've been standing here and instead of helping us you just sit there. How do you justify your job?"

"I'm here to make sure no one steals anything," said Moron. "Did you steal anything? No? Okay, I've done my job." For emphasis he patted himself on the back for a job well done.

"That's only part of your job! What about the customer service?" said the woman.

"How do you know what my job requires? Have you read my job description?"

"No, but . . ."

"Then shut up. Leave the damn store."

"You know," said Gary. "The timer still says eighteen minutes. You got nothing better to do. Might as well help us."

"Perfect," said Moron, standing up. "That means I have time to head to the bathroom and grab a snack." He smacks another button. The feminine voice said, "Attention everyone. Due to technical difficulties, we request that everyone set down the trinkets they were planning on buying and exit the store in an orderly fashion. This is not a drill. Please don't panic." The rest of the patrons in the store put their things down and left the store. Gary and the couple were unmoved.

"I can't leave until you three leave. So get out," said Moron.

"Well I guess you're stuck, because I'm not leaving," said Gary.

"We aren't either," said Jenny.

"But honey, is it really that impor-"

"We're not leaving!"

"Fine. I'm going over to look at the stuffed animals, though."

"Alright, you win," said Moron. "Guess I have to help you." He looked down at the tickets. They said Infinite Fun Zone, but with an unfamiliar, old-fashioned logo. The date on them said 2002. "Paper tickets? Okay that's your problem right there. Everything is digital now. The tickets are tied to your identity chip."

"They're still perfectly valid! I earned them from this very place fifty years ago!" said Gary.

"Well then, you should have picked up that stupid plastic pink unicorn fifty years ago, because we don't accept them anymore."

"You didn't have this then. And I haven't been around for fifty years to be able to redeem them. I've been . . . away."

"Wow, fifty years; where did you go? Pluto or something?" said Jenny with interest. "I hear it's been nice the past thirty or so years. Relatively speaking, of course."

"Might as well have been. I was in prison."

Moron's level of interest in the man immediately rose a few notches above nonexistent. "Prison? That's cool. Do they still initiate new blood by pinning them to the wall and etching a caricature onto their backs with shivs, or is that just an exaggeration perpetrated by Bollywood?"

"Either that's an exaggeration, or they must not have realized I was new blood until it was too late, because my back is distinctly lacking in caricature. I can prove it if you like." Gary began pulling the tail of his shirt out of the waist of his pants.

199

"No!" said Moron. "Let's leave it a mystery."

Gary tucked his shirt back in. "I had no intention of showing you my wrinkles and moles anyway."

Moron did not want to leave every mystery unsolved, though, so he asked, "Why did you go to prison?"

"I heard they had lovely gardens and simply had to find out for myself," said Gary. "No, I went the same way everyone else does. I committed a crime."

Jenny backed away a few steps, no longer quite as sure of this old man. "What for?"

"In order to accurately convey what happened I need to tell a somewhat lengthy story. One that lasts about," he glanced at his timer, "ten minutes, as it so happens."

"Go ahead," said Moron. "I know you jerks are going to force me to sit around doing absolutely nothing otherwise anyway."

The man came back from his prize research. "Honey, I think if you'll just listen to reason and put away the talking keychain, I can get the giant foam rockstar hands, and we'd still have enough left over that you could get the Siamese twins monkey puppet you said was cute."

"Quiet. He's about to tell us about prison." And with that she latches on to his arm and positioned him so that if Gary turned out to be a knife-wielding serial killer, she could quickly pull her husband's chest into the path of the knife blade in place of her own.

Gary began his story:

"While in prison I started writing a screenplay based on my story, with only some mild embellishments here and there that tweak my personality into that of an awesome and enviable person, so I don't want to give too much away or risk spoiling your future movie-going experience."

"But here's the short version: I went from being a video rental clerk to being pinned to my bed by a group of large, sweaty, and uniformed men in just a few months. I used the technical knowledge of some geek as well as my own knowledge of human psychology to make a website that was better at getting people to happily hand over their life savings than a casino would. It was legal. They got me on tax evasion charges only by passing a law overnight that required any companies with four or less employees and generating a billion dollars of income a month to file taxes eight months and fourteen days early. I didn't even get the chance to rub the crust out of my eyes that morning."

"The police high-fived each other and smacked each other's butts after they got me, the jury snarled at me during the proceedings, and the judge gave me the 'I'm going to slit your throat' gesture even before he looked at the verdict."

"Prison was mostly boring, but we'll spice it up for the movie because "Oz" made the idea of prison being Hell on Earth a requirement. Maybe in the movie I'll even get that shiv caricature on my back."

"However, there was one guy there I will never forget. Sergeant Dribbles we called him. At first it was because I found him disgusting, since saliva oozed out of his mouth whenever he talked. In time, though, he became my best friend, and we would play games of Chutes N' Ladders in our heads. The game was banned, you see, since the plastic spinner could be fashioned into a shiv."

"One day he let me in on his big secret; the one thing that made him soft and vulnerable, something that you're never supposed to tell anyone in the clink."

"He told me that his daughter on the outside, desperately waiting for her birthday present, and he was afraid that if he got it to her more than six months late, that she would resent him and teach him a lesson by not rebelling against him in her teen years, instead following all of the bad advice he'd taught her, and thus end up killing someone like he did and ruining her life."

"I bet you can guess what that present was by now, can't you? A plastic, pink unicorn."

"Aww," said Jenny, clutching her man tighter.

Moron scratched his chin. "I see where this is going. He entrusted you with it since you were getting out soon, somehow you lost it or probably something dramatic happened that involved its destruction, and you vowed to get it to her, and what a coincidence, the pink plastic unicorns here just happen to be exactly like the one the guy had in prison."

"You aren't the son of one of the few Bollywood agents I sent an advance copy of the script to, are you? That's pretty much exactly how it goes. Not how it happened in real life, of course, but that's how audiences will want to see the story."

"I don't buy it. It's too corny," said the man. "Sounds like a cable network's 'Movie of the Week' at best."

"Again," said Gary. "Not like how it happened in real life. Plus I'd be satisfied with Movie of the Week for my first go. I can always try for a "Shawshank Redemption" after I finally become successful."

"Weren't you already successful once though? Billion dollars a month successful?" asked Jenny.

"Um. Yeah but- you see, it was all taken away from me before I even got to use it."

"Still, wouldn't you say 'successful again', not 'finally successful'?"

"Um. No, because . . . you see, it – it didn't really count, because I only spent like, a million dollars of it before they caught me, which is really nothing at all, really. It only buys a mansion, and go karts, and a fancy diamond necklace, and a grid of televisions, and-"

"Actually it only buys a weekend in Hawaii now," said Jenny, folding her arms across her chest. "But you got that from the movie "Blank Check". We were forced to watch that in my sociology class because it exemplified early American consumption."

"You just got trapped in a lie," said Moron. "So what did you really do in prison? Become a pathetic drug addict who debased himself to feed his addiction?"

"What's with you insisting I must be this awful person?" asked Gary. "You must really be a sad person yourself in order to-

Jenny squealed and pointed an accusatory finger at Gary. "Ooh, he's deflecting the accusation! Refusing to answer directly!"

The man said, "Dead giveaway. He's a big fat liar, he is."

Gary started backing away from everyone like they were all infected with the same contagious disease. "Let's just calm down. You all are getting way too excited. I can explain everything."

"You can explain everything? The guilty always say that!" said Moron. He leapt over the counter and moved in for the kill.

"You three would make an excellent jury," muttered Gary quietly. He edged up dangerously close to the exit, where the electric anti-
theft device laid waiting to demobilize anyone who tried to leave with store property. "I just have one thing to ask you, Moron. After having heard this story will you let me take this unicorn to Sergeant Dribbles' daughter, free of charge?"

"Absolutely not," said Moron.

"That's all I needed to hear. You all can stop moving in on me like psychopaths, I can tell the truth now."

They paused, but still remained tensed and ready to pounce.

"You three are correct. I was just telling you all a bit of a fib there. It's a story I had to memorize for my line of work. I prepare for a lot of detours, but I wasn't expecting that one, so you managed to trip me up. Congratulations."

Each of the three relax and looked at each other with a smug look on their faces. Moron gave himself another pat on the back, then said, "What line of work?"

"Glad you asked," said Gary. "Infinite Fun Zone wants to insure a high level of customer service, so they periodically hire people to test the staff. I'm proud to say, Mr. Moron, that you failed with flying colors!"

"Oh come on, you tried to redeem paper tickets! We don't accept them, end of story."

"Wrong! It clearly says in the handbook that you are to accommodate people who have paper tickets. Also page 22 says not to be a jerk and ignore the customer until they force you to acknowledge them."

"The handbook? I deleted that right after they Mindlinked it to me. You can't expect me to listen to anything so boring for more than two minutes. Besides, what about you? You look like you're 100 years old! Shouldn't you have retired a decade ago, old man?"

The woman squealed and pointed an accusatory finger at Moron. "Ooh, he's deflecting the accusation! Refusing to answer directly!"

The man said, "Dead giveaway. He's a lazy, horrible employee, he is."

"Cool it," said Gary. "Actually I'm only 30. And I only look like I'm 70, thank you very much."

"You're a college student?" asked Jenny. "How did you – oh wait, you're an Ager, aren't you? I heard about them, but hadn't met any."

"Well now you have," said Gary.

Moron laughed. "I'd never do anything so stupid like that. They don't have any way to reverse it yet, you know. You're stuck with that old, wrinkly skin. Good luck getting women."

"I do just fine with women, thank you," said Gary. "And you have to do whatever you can to get job experience in this economy. You'll find out how bad it's gotten before too long."

"I've worked here for ten years. They haven't fired me for tons of stupid stuff, so they won't fire me over a stupid unicorn."

"Care to make a bet on that?" asked Gary.

"Not really."

"Good. It's not too late to give me excellent customer service, you know."

"How?"

"Just press whatever button that will let me leave this place unharmed."

"Fine. Done." He turned back to the counter and pressed a button. The lights in the room suddenly dimmed, with a spotlight shining on Gary's face. The feminine said into their voice chips, "Attention everyone. We must have a celebrity with us today, as we're doing the unthinkable and giving him something for free! Everyone feel free to harass this person and bug him for autographs!"

206

"Thank you," said Gary to Moron. He raised the unicorn up near his lips and whispered, "Let's get you to Isabella before it's too late." He fiddled with his timer, disabled the MiniEMP device on the View 2000, grabbed it, then quickly turned and ran out the store.

"Well that was weird," said Jenny. Her companion nodded. To Mr. Moron, who was already back in his seat and turning on his View 2000 again, she said, "Okay, can you help us out now?"

Mr. Moron reached out for a button on the Employee EZ Answer Sheet, but hesitated before pressing it. "Um, sure, I can help you, valued customer or potential mystery shopper. But could you wait thirty or so minutes while I hunt down and listen to the employee handbook first?"

Infinite Monkeys

Made in the USA
Charleston, SC
08 December 2009